"I don't have to answer to you, Jake!"

His eyes blazed. "How true," he said thinly. "But there is one thing you have to do for me, like it or not. You're still legally married to me.... I think you know what I'm talking about."

A shiver of alarm ran through her as he caught her arm. "That won't solve anything, Jake," Laura said breathlessly, staring at the hand on her wrist.

He gave a mocking laugh that turned her spine to ice. "I don't give a damn if it solves anything! I find it far more pleasant than arguing with you. I've been patient with you long enough, Laura. It's time you stopped running."

Her eyes riveted on his face, she noticed immediately his look of triumph as he moved closer to her.

SARAH HOLLAND
is also the author of this

Harlequin Presents

516—TOO HOT TO HANDLE

SARAH HOLLAND

tomorrow began yesterday

Harlequin Books

TORONTO • NEW YORK • LOS ANGELES • LONDON
AMSTERDAM • PARIS • SYDNEY • HAMBURG
STOCKHOLM • ATHENS • TOKYO • MILAN

For
Gudi Mohal, Janet and Gary,
Diane and Paul, and Michael O'Connell

Harlequin Presents first edition October 1982
ISBN 0-373-10536-3

Original hardcover edition published in 1982
by Mills & Boon Limited

CHAPTER ONE

LAURA surveyed the crowded nightclub with amused green eyes. It was close to midnight now, and she couldn't help but wonder as to what might happen on the witching hour. Maybe she would turn into a pumpkin. She laughed softly, thinking that perhaps life would be easier if she were turned into a pumpkin, because what no one at her table knew was that tonight was her wedding anniversary. Neither did they know that she had ever been married.

She wound a strand of her silky red-gold hair around one finger and tugged on it almost childishly. One year ago today, she thought, her pale pink lips pursed reflectively. Her eyes fell on her now bare left hand, and she sat for a moment, staring at it, isolated from the noise and laughter all around her. Then she picked up her drink, sipped it, and shrugged her thoughts away.

Rupert leaned over, beaming from ear to ear. 'Enjoying yourself, Laura?' he asked, his thin, hollow face wreathed in smiles, the top of his greying head slightly balding, stray hairs hanging over his forehead.

Laura smiled, nodding. 'Lovely, Rupert, thanks.'

'Oh, good, good,' he said, one hand patting her paternally. Rupert was the editor of the magazine Laura worked for, and tonight was his birthday.

'Good, good,' he repeated once more. He wasn't exactly a great conversationalist. He searched around for something else to say.

Laura took pity on him. 'She's a good singer, isn't

she?' She nodded towards the girl who sang at the front of the club, her strident voice echoing round the room.

Rupert looked relieved. 'Oh yes, excellent, excellent.'

Laura had hoped that her comment might have prompted him into further conversation. She glanced at his anxious face and a smile of resignation touched her lips. Rupert was stumped.

His eyes darted around, alighting on the champagne bottle. He picked it up with an inspired look. 'More champagne, Laura?' he queried, waving the bottle haphazardly over her glass.

She placed a slim hand over the mouth of her glass, shaking her head. 'Not for me—goes straight to my head, champagne.'

'Best place for it,' said Rupert, feeling he had made a joke. He laughed heartily, and the rest of the staff joined in, not wishing to offend him. People always laughed when Rupert laughed.

Laura studied his face affectionately. He was rather sweet. The drawn tired lines of his face were so often lit up with laughter that one could easily forget just how stern he could be when the situation called for it.

He was very successful as the editor of a women's magazine. He seemed to know instinctively what a woman would like to read about—a rare quality for a man, Laura reflected. He certainly got on well with all the female staff, and they all loved him. But he was also a very good editor, and a very fair man.

Laura had been working for *Style* for a year now, and was more than happy with her job there. The atmosphere was lighthearted, and the pay was just enough to keep her happily in her little flat. When she had first joined, she had been wary of working in a London-based office, knowing how easy it would be to be recognised. But it hadn't happened yet, and she wasn't going to draw attention to herself in any way.

She didn't usually accompany her colleagues on their regular nights out. She didn't enjoy sitting at a table for hours, waiting for the next jet-setter to arrive. She preferred to stay at home with a good book.

When she had first joined the magazine, her striking good looks had attracted a lot of attention from the male staff. The riot of curly, shoulder length red-gold hair which surrounded her enchantingly pretty face with laughing green eyes and a full pink mouth had been a hit on the first day. But after a few polite refusals, the message had gradually filtered through the office grapevine: Laura was not interested.

She leaned back in her seat, her eyes wandering leisurely over the diners. This was an exclusive place—the fact made obvious by the lack of prices.

'Dead giveaway,' Carly had drawled beside her as they studied the menus.

Carly was the Assistant Features Editor. A cynical, glamorous twenty-eight-year-old, she had been working for *Style* since leaving school. Her interests, according to Carly, were men and money—in that order.

She tapped her long, red-tipped fingers on the table. 'All taken, as usual,' she drawled.

Laura turned her head. 'Sorry?' she asked with a frown.

Carly's eyes held wry amusement as they slid towards Laura. 'Men, my dear, men.' Her glance flicked back across the nightclub, searching for someone who pleased her. 'They all seem to be out with their ladies tonight.'

Laura grinned. Carly had a one-track mind. But then she had never been married. She wasn't as cynical as she would have people believe. Laura had the idea that Carly was looking for her Waterloo.

Carly leaned back in her seat with an elegant ripple of silk. 'Get me a drink, Stephen,' she said in a husky, commanding tone, and the young man opposite jumped up to obey, his young face eager and admiring.

Carly smiled like a Cheshire cat. 'At least someone appreciates me!'

Laura grinned, sipping her drink. 'Hang on in there, Carly old friend. You'll strike lucky one day.'

Carly raised a perfectly plucked eyebrow. 'When I'm about ninety-three.'

Laura detected a note of sadness in her voice, but she didn't comment. Carly was not the sort to share her troubles, and neither was Laura. They understood each other, and worked well together. But although they were good friends, soul-baring didn't come into their relationship.

Laura noticed Stephen staring soulfully at Carly and smiled to herself. He was a little too young—Carly preferred her men well seasoned.

They were silent for a moment, then Carly nudged her sharply, her red-tipped fingers resting on the table. 'Who,' she drawled, admiringly, 'is that?'

Laura glanced round and followed her gaze.

A sudden tremor ran through her as she met a pair of piercing blue eyes, watching her through half-lowered lids. His attractive, tanned face was carved on harsh lines, the hard controlled mouth was sensual, and a slight smile curved it as he inclined his black head, acknowledging her.

She looked away. 'Jake Ashton,' she said with a bite.

Carly looked surprised. 'You don't like?'

Laura shook her head grimly. 'I don't like.'

'He is what I call edible,' Carly drawled, her red mouth curling.

'Give him a bite from me,' snapped Laura.

Carly glanced at her then, and her eyes narrowed into slits as she studied her closely. 'Nasty,' she commented, her voice half amused. 'Do I take it he's not your type?'

Laura remained silent. Not my type at all, she thought. Most definitely not. I don't go in for cruel bastards. But the shock of seeing that arrogant face after so long was too much for her. Slowly she turned her head to look at him.

Their eyes locked in a silent duel. Laura had to admit he was still an extremely sexy man, with the look of a sleek, powerful animal, his body lithe and hard. But her thoughts did not show in her face; the mask she had built up for that purpose was too deeply ingrained. Slowly, she ran her eyes over the length of his body, from his head to his toe. She flicked her glance back to his face, her contemptuous stare conveying the message, that she found him sadly lacking.

He raised one jet-black brow and smiled, his mouth insolent, and angry colour swept into her face. She looked away quickly.

Carly leant over to her a moment later. 'He's coming over,' she drawled. 'And sweetie, he's looking at you. Let me know if you get bored with him. I'd love to see him on my breakfast tray!'

Laura's head came up sharply. Jake Ashton was walking across to them, the tall streamlined body carrying the lazy grace of a panther; magnetic but lethal.

Her heart began to thud in disturbed, crazy movements against her chest. She swallowed on a suddenly dry throat. Why was he coming over? Was he going to tell them, break her secret to her colleagues?

She knew he was watching her, and her eyes flashed to his face. The black dinner jacket was cut superbly, showing his broad shoulders to perfection. His muscular thighs were outlined in the dark material, and she felt a sharp sense of longing which she pushed angrily out of sight. She did not want to be reminded of her sexual feelings for this man. All he had ever done was ruin her life.

Carly eyed him with a predatory smile. 'Hello,' she said with emphasis.

He inclined his black head and smiled lazily.

'Good evening,' he said in a dark voice.

Carly flashed her pretty white teeth at him.

Rupert jumped to his feet, 'Jake, my dear fellow!' he spluttered, extending one thin hand.

Jake took the proffered hand. 'Rupert. How are you?'

'Oh, marvellous, marvellous!' Rupert burbled, his face wreathed in smiles.

Laura's face was deliberately blank as she watched this exchange. She hated Jake for his smooth, easy charm, the way people jumped to do his bidding when he crooked a finger. She despised his confidence; he behaved as though he were a God, and expected others to view him in this light also.

'Perform the introductions, Rupert dear,' Carly drawled irritably from beside her.

Laura didn't lift her head, but she could feel Jake Ashton's gaze searing through her. She studiously ignored him.

Jake switched the powerful charm of his smile to Carly's face. The introductions were performed, and Laura kept a tight rein on her temper as she heard the dark, sensual voice drawing exactly the right reaction from Carly.

She slid a glance at her from beneath her lashes, and was faintly irritated to see the other girl preening herself like a well-fed pussycat.

Rupert was fussing about all over the place. 'Won't you sit down, Jake? Join us for a while.' He peered at Jake with the utmost sincerity. 'We would be honoured if you would join us for a glass of champagne.'

Jake didn't appear to need much persuasion. He sat down in the chair opposite Laura, stretching his long legs smoothly before him. 'Thank you.'

Rupert noticed Jake's interest in Laura. She saw it in his thin face, and gritted her teeth. Rupert was beginning to get on her nerves.

'Laura,' he blustered, beaming with pride, 'I would like you to meet Jake Ashton. Jake, this is one of our assistants in Features, Laura Hadleigh.'

She looked up in time to see the imperceptible narrowing of his eyes. His brows pulled together in a frown as he studied her. She knew what was on his mind, but he could go to hell before she acknowledged it.

She looked at him squarely, her face cold. 'Mr Ashton,' she said shortly.

He offered her a lean, tanned hand. Laura ignored it. She heard a polite cough beside her, and looked up into Rupert's frowning face. Her lips tightened, her glance flicking back to Jake. If he insisted on polite formalities, that was what he would get, and no more.

His grip was cool and firm, and she forced down the sudden acceleration of her heart. 'Good evening,' she said in a clipped, polite voice.

The blue eyes held hers. 'Miss Hadleigh.'

She felt herself breath out with relief. For one terrifying moment, she had thought he might tell them, but for some reason of his own he had chosen to remain silent. Why? I'll find out later, no doubt, she thought grimly. Jake would not let it pass without comment. I'll just have to stay out of his way, she decided.

She tried to withdraw her hand, but he held on to it. He studied her coolly, his face thoughtful. She was about to pull her hand hard away from him, when he let go, very gently. Laura averted her eyes quickly from the mocking smile which curved his mouth. She picked up her glass and sipped her drink as calmly as she could manage.

Rupert leaned over. 'Jake's in television, you know,' he said confidingly, nodding his grey head at her.

Laura twirled the glass in her hand. 'Really?' she said in a flat, bored voice.

Jake studied her for a moment, then he leaned back in his seat. 'You of all people should know that,' he said softly.

Her heart stopped fractionally. Was he going to tell them? She leaned forward. 'Why do you say that?'

His mouth curved in a cruel smile. He knew what was running through her mind, and her lips tightened.

He was going to hold her on the end of a thread for the rest of the evening.

He tilted his head to one side. 'Because we're both in the media business.'

Laura glared at him resentfully. You bastard, she thought, you're enjoying this. There was nothing he liked more than playing intricate games with people's fears and emotions. Beneath that charming smile lay a brain of cold, shrewd cunning. He could pick up the scent of fear in seconds, and knew exactly how to play on it.

Rupert nodded at Laura again, his face knowledge-able. 'Oh yes, Jake's very big in the States.'

Laura was not impressed. 'How fascinating!'

Rupert looked worried. 'He's quite important here, too, Laura,' he said, obviously trying to prompt her into showing more respect. But Laura would not be prompted.

She raised an eyebrow at Jake, her face deliberately insolent. 'A big fish in a little pool?'

'Some might even say, a shark, Miss Hadleigh,' he said softly.

The softness of that dark voice sent shivers running through her body. But she saw no reason why she should pander to his almighty ego and treat him with the respect normally reserved for visiting royalty.

She eyed him with distaste. 'I've always thought sharks were rather ugly creatures.'

'They are also extremely dangerous,' he said silkily.

There was a little silence. Rupert coughed, his eyes darting from Jake to Laura. He looked about him at the rest of the staff for guidance, then his face lit up with an idea and he reached into his jacket, pulling out a case which he opened, and offered to Jake.

'A cigar, Jake?' he asked with a hopeful smile.

'Thank you.' Jake selected a cigar.

Rupert leaned over with a slim gold lighter, holding the flame to Jake's cigar. Jake's eyes were narrowed against the silver-blue smoke as it curled from the glowing tip of the cigar. His mouth closed over it in a strong movement, and he watched Laura coolly through the haze of smoke.

Rupert cleared his throat. 'How are things at N.T.N.?' he asked, leaning forward with interest.

'Running smoothly,' Jake told him, tapping the ash from the end of his cigar into an ashtray. 'Even though I'm not there to keep an eye on them at the moment.'

'And what brings you to London?' Rupert queried.

'Two things.' Jake rested one long hand on the table. 'The deal with one of the British Networks. That should be cleared up by the end of the month. Also, we're signing up Theresa Phillips for another couple of years.'

Rupert frowned thoughtfully. 'I thought she was still in the States.'

He shook his head. 'She flew back for a short break.'

'If she knows you're going to be signing her up again, why are you here? Why not wait until she comes back?' Rupert asked, his grey head tilted to one side.

'She likes attention,' said Jake, his eyes flickering to Laura's face.

She eyed him irritably. 'And you're here to give it to her.'

He smiled slowly. 'Among other things,' he murmured.

Her teeth clamped together. He really ought to get

together with Carly. The two of them had one thing in common—they both had an insatiable desire for the opposite sex. She remembered his main failing almost too clearly. It had nearly broken her in two.

'Of course,' she gave him a blistering smile, her voice sweet and honeyed, 'you're very good at that sort of thing, aren't you?'

A smile tugged at the corners of his mouth. 'Thank you.'

She hadn't meant it as a compliment, and he knew it. She had flung it at him as an insult, and he had deliberately misunderstood her words. But that was typical of Jake. She should have known better than to play word games with him; he was too damned clever.

Rupert was still beaming at Jake. 'How is Theresa?' he sipped his drink. 'Haven't seen much of her lately.'

'We've kept her working pretty hard. She hasn't had time for filming in this country. This is the first real break she's had,' Jake told him.

Rupert toyed with his glass. 'Pretty little thing, Theresa. Always thought she was pretty.'

'Yes,' Jake shot a mocking glance at Laura, 'she's ravishing. It makes my job easier. I prefer persuading beautiful women to work with me, they're so much more enjoyable than tired executives.'

You don't have to tell me that, she thought bitterly as she looked at him, I know you of old. She looked away almost immediately. She didn't want him to see the sudden flash of bitter anger in her eyes. Whatever happened, she must maintain the barrier, he mustn't guess at her inner feelings. If Jake Ashton got the chance, he would smash her into tiny pieces again, and she wasn't going to give him that chance. Not if she could help it.

Carly caught her eye, and bent her head to speak in a hushed drawl to Laura. 'What gives?'

Laura's eyes held wry amusement. Everyone at the table had picked up the atmosphere between herself and Jake, but she hadn't expected anyone to question her on it. Most of the staff normally let her go her own way without question, giving her the occasional enquiring glance, but saying nothing.

Carly's red mouth curved. 'Don't keep me in suspense, will you?' she said drily.

Laura looked down at her hands. 'I just don't like him very much,' she said, and it wasn't far from the truth.

If she had expected Carly to fall for that, she would have been a fool. But Carly took the point, and leaned back elegantly, one slim hand resting on the table. 'No comment?' she asked with a wry smile.

Laura shook her head.

Carly shrugged. 'Thought so.' Her predatory eyes darted towards Jake, who was talking to Rupert, his black head averted to one side.

Laura knew he was listening. He was only too well aware of their conversation, although he showed no signs of it. Jake's bland mask fell into place as easily as that of a poker player's.

Carly tilted her head to one side. Her eyes narrowed slightly as she studied Laura. 'You know him, don't you?' she observed shrewdly. 'And you know him very well, too.'

Laura raised her head. She looked at Carly squarely, her face bland, and did not reply.

Carly shrugged, 'Okay, I can take a hint, sweetie.'

Her mouth lifted at the corner and she raised an eye-brow in resignation.

The music began playing, and couples drifted on to the dance floor. Jake glanced briefly in the direction of the dancing, then he looked back at Laura.

Her heart jerked in sheer panic. If she had to dance with him, she would be putting herself at risk. Her mind worked quickly. She stood up, looking at Rupert.

'Come on,' she said hurriedly, taking his arm, 'it's your birthday. You get the first dance.'

Rupert looked pleased. Jake, on the other hand, did not. His eyes stabbed at her, but she avoided them. Rupert beamed at all and sundry, and patted Laura on the arm, leading her off to the dance floor.

She breathed a silent sigh of relief. Rupert put his hand on her waist, and held her other hand as they began dancing in time to the music. She glanced back at the table and stiffened. Carly and Jake were walking arm in arm on to the dance floor.

Something clutched at her heart, dragging it into the pit of her stomach. Jealous, she thought angrily, I'm jealous of her. She watched as Jake's strong arms closed around Carly, and he began moving sensuously against her.

Laura felt sick. After all this time she could still feel physical pain when she saw him with another woman. The realisation made her angry with herself, and she pushed the feeling down, turning away from the sight of them.

Rupert shuffled about on the dance floor. 'What do you think of Jake, then, Laura?'

She looked up at him. 'Off the top of my head?' she queried wryly.

Rupert frowned. 'Er . . . yes.'

'To tell the truth, Rupert, I don't really like him at all.'

He looked amazed, as though it was unheard of to dislike someone as powerful as Jake Ashton. 'But why?'

'I occasionally take a dislike to some people,' she lied. 'He just happens to be one of them.'

Rupert was scandalised. 'But, Laura, he's terribly important!'

'What's that got to do with it?' she asked irritably. 'Hitler was important, and nobody liked him.'

They moved around on the dance floor, the soft music filling the air. 'That's different, Laura.'

'Why is it? Is there a law about it?'

'No.' He shuffled uncomfortably. 'But you do have to be very careful with these network heads, they have very delicate egos, you know.'

She eyed him wryly. 'Don't make me laugh! His ego's about as delicate as a steel vault.'

'Oh no,' he assured her earnestly, 'you're quite mistaken.'

'Do me a favour, Rupert. You couldn't shatter Jake Ashton's ego with a nuclear attack.'

The music stopped, bringing an end to their conversation, and Laura began to walk back in the direction of their table. She felt Rupert nudge her discreetly, and turned her head.

Jake and Carly were standing behind them, Carly draped over Jake's arm, her red mouth curved with pleasure.

Jake studied her with a casual smile. 'Would you

excuse me?' he murmured, and Carly's hand slid off his arm in a languorous movement.

Laura stiffened. She could read him like a book. 'I'm rather thirsty,' she announced, turning to Rupert. 'Shall we go back to the table? I can ask the waiter to bring me some water.'

Rupert shrugged. 'I don't see why not,' he muttered uncertainly.

Jake took her arm deftly. 'I'll see to that.' He eyed Rupert. 'Escort Carly back to the table for me.'

Carly's lips twisted in a resigned grimace. She grudgingly returned Jake's charming smile, then turned to Rupert. 'Come on, Buster,' she said, taking his arm, 'you and me have got to take a little walk.'

They glided away, leaving Jake alone with Laura. His glance flickered quickly over her slender body, taking in the slim waist and full, rounded breasts. 'Shall we dance?'

Her lips tightened. She didn't appear to have much choice. 'If you insist,' she said in a clipped, cold voice.

'I do.' His fingers slid around her waist in a slow movement, pulling her gently against him as he began to move slowly in time to the music. Laura felt her heartbeat accelerate as their bodies touched. She held herself away from him, trying to prevent contact as much as possible. Her back was stiff and unyielding, and she stared fixedly at a point just past his shoulder.

Jake looked down at her, his mouth twitching with amusement. The strong fingers slid to her hips, and he pulled her harder against him. Laura stiffened further as she felt his thighs brushing hers in strong, silky movements.

She didn't look at him. 'Stop it,' she told him in a cold voice.

'Stop what?' he murmured against her hair, caressing her hips slowly. His thighs pressed against hers sensuously, and she felt a sudden rush of heat flood her body.

Her heart began to thud jerkily. 'Would you please get your hands off me?'

'No.' His hands slid slowly up and down her back. 'I'm enjoying myself too much.'

'I hate to be the one to smash your monumental ego,' she muttered through clenched teeth, 'but I am *not* enjoying *my*self.'

He drew his head back to look at her. 'You still bite, I see.'

'Yes,' she snapped. 'Very hard!'

He laughed softly, drawing her back against him.

'Good,' he murmured, 'you always excited me with your teeth.'

The hot colour swept through her face, and she bit deep into her lip. She should have seen that one coming. If you stand in the way of a train, you must expect it to knock you down.

She fell into an acid silence for a moment, then she felt his breath fan her neck through the silky curtain of her hair. His lips brushed swiftly against her skin, and heat coursed through her, making her legs weak and her heart pound faster.

She jerked her head back. 'Don't do that!'

'Why?' Jake murmured. 'Don't you like it?' His head bent quickly, his mouth brushing hers. Her blood-pressure shot up. He lifted his head to look at her, and she saw the glitter in his eyes.

'No, I don't like it.' Her hands curled into fists on his shoulders. 'Why you should imagine that I do defeats me.'

'Really?' The lean brown fingers rested on the top of her breasts before she could stop him. His face was insolent. 'Your heart's going like a steam hammer. Excitement—or fear?'

She sucked in her breath. 'Your head should be on exhibition at the British Museum!' she told him acidly.

He raised one eyebrow. 'What an interesting idea.'

'You are the most . . .' she began.

His hand bit into her wrist cruelly. 'And you,' he drawled, 'are becoming very rude.'

'That's what's known as tough luck. Nobody asked you to dance with me.'

He smiled thinly. 'True. But I couldn't resist holding your sexy little body in my arms. Brings back memories.'

Her eyes flashed to his dark, forbidding face. It brought back a lot of memories to her too. But then she didn't have to be in Jake's arms to recall the feel of him—her thoughts had been occupied by him for longer than she cared to remember. Every time her mind conjured up that image, that tableau, which she had witnessed a year ago, she felt the same aching, physical pain well up sharply inside her. No, she didn't want to have to go through that again; she would cut her throat first.

'You may want a trip down memory lane,' she said in a cold voice, 'but I can do without it, thank you very much.'

His face grew darker, and his hand tightened on her

wrist. 'Prefer to forget?' he queried icily. 'Or had you already forgotten?'

She caught the angry glitter of his eyes. But she knew what she was doing. There was no way on this earth that she would admit to the endless, sleepless nights to be laid at his door. She looked at him squarely. 'I'd already forgotten.'

His mouth straightened into a firm, hard line. She felt his powerful muscles tauten beneath her fingertips, rippling beneath the smooth material. They danced in silence, moving on the floor slowly as the music filled the air with a haunting melody.

Jake didn't look at her when he spoke. 'Am I so forgettable, Laura?' he murmured.

She felt the brush of his lips against her cheek as his black head bent, and she said in a chilly voice, 'Different tactics? They won't work, you know. You killed off everything I felt for you a year ago.' She ignored the dangerous tensing of his body, and drew her head back to eye him with icy indifference. 'You're wasting your time.'

The music stopped, and she broke away from him, turning to walk back to her table, but his hand shot out, clamping around her wrist like a steel vice.

She looked at her arm pointedly. 'May I have my arm back? Unless you'd rather keep it as a souvenir. You could always pin it up over a doorway or stick it on your belt.'

The blue eyes ran lazily over the length of her body before flickering back up to her face. 'I'd much rather keep the rest of you,' he said with a cruel smile. 'Your arm wouldn't be much use to me in bed.'

Hot colour flooded her face. 'Your obsession with sex disgusts me!'

'Too bad,' he said with a bite. 'You're just going to have to be disgusted and put up with it.'

She knew that to get away from him, she would have to put up an undignified struggle in full view of everyone in the nightclub. That was not her idea of fun, and he knew it. He knew she would rather go with him than draw attention to herself in that way.

'Let me go!' She pulled at her wrist.

'No way, honey.' His face was grim, carved on dangerous lines. 'I think it's time you and I had a little talk.'

He flicked her wrist, pulling her after him as he strode across the floor towards the balcony, and Laura stumbled after him, her eyes flaring as she glared at the back of his black head.

They reached the balcony, and the fresh air was sweet-smelling and warm, the summer night drawing out the perfume of the flowers set around the balcony. Jake marched her across to the far side of the balcony, his long legs carrying him way ahead of Laura.

'I don't want to talk to you!' she hissed as he stopped, turning to face her. 'We have nothing to say to each other.'

His face tightened. 'Like I said; too bad. You'll just have to grin and bear it. You ran away last time, and this time I'm going to make sure you stay and listen to what I have to say.'

She tried to pull her wrist out of his grasp. 'I'm not interested in your pathetic excuses. I didn't believe you then, and I see no reason why I should change my mind.'

His eyes glittered dangerously, his hand clamping

her against him in a harsh, painful movement. 'You stubborn little bitch!' he bit out. 'You'll do as you're damned well told!'

Laura struggled furiously against him, aware that her struggle was totally ineffectual against his determined strength. 'Who in God's name do you think you are?' she flung. 'Don't try to pull the Great Dictator number on me! You're not Mussolini!'

'No, I'm not.' His voice cracked like a whip. 'I'm your husband.'

CHAPTER TWO

HER struggles ceased at his words, and she eyed him bitterly. 'A fact I would prefer to forget!'

His hands were biting into her wrists, and he pulled them in a swift movement behind her back, pinning her against him, until she found she couldn't move even if she tried. 'I'm sure you would,' he snarled, his lips drawn back over his teeth. 'Unfortunately there's very little you can do about it—except divorce me.'

'What a good idea!'

A cruel smile curved his mouth. 'I don't think so. You know better than to try fighting me in court. I'd make sure you came out bleeding all over the floor.'

Her lips tightened. He was right, of course. She hated admitting it, but he was right. She would never dare to risk a battle in court with him. Jake would pull no punches, hold no compassion if she tried to take him on. He could be a ruthless bastard when he wanted to be, and he didn't need the slightest provocation if he thought someone was trying to get the better of him. It came as second nature to him.

He studied her, his head tilted to one side in a way which she remembered only too clearly. 'And of course, annulment is quite out of the question. Don't you think?'

She wanted to slap his handsome, smiling face. Her feelings must have shown through to her eyes, because he tightened his grip on her and shook his head grimly.

'Don't try it,' he warned. 'I'll slap you back, twice as hard.'

Her eyes flared. 'I believe you. You're quite capable of hitting a woman. I wouldn't be surprised if you enjoyed it!'

His fingers bit into her flesh. 'I don't make a habit of it,' he snarled, 'but I do make exceptions to my rules. And, lady, you are one exception I'm going to enjoy making if you don't watch your language.'

A shudder ran through her, chilling her spine as she caught the danger lying in his words. He was stronger than she was, and he could easily hurt her without any effort at all.

She stared at him in bitter distaste. 'Go ahead, beat me up. I'm sure you'd enjoy it far more than merely talking to me,' she spat. 'That's how you get your kicks, isn't it?'

His hands twisted her arms higher up her back, pushing her forward against him, her breasts resting on his chest. His eyes flicked down over them, and he pushed her further against him, his thighs pressing against hers.

A smile curved his mouth. 'That's where you're wrong. This is how I get my kicks.'

His eyes burned on her lips, and the black head swooped down, taking her mouth in a bruising, punishing kiss. Laura struggled bitterly, her arms pulling uselessly against his superior strength. His mouth forced her lips back against her teeth, and she tasted the salty flow of blood on her tongue.

Her heart was thudding dangerously, an overwhelming heat hitting her like a steam-train. Her mind screamed out in protest against the long-forgotten sensations Jake was arousing in her body. She continued to struggle against him, refusing to give in to her own desires.

He drew his head back, breathing harshly, and stared down at her with a brooding expression. His face was a deep red underneath his tan, and the blue glitter of his eyes held a sexual intensity which she preferred to forget.

'I could get to like hurting you, Laura,' he muttered. 'Your struggles only excite me.'

Laura was so angry, she thought the top of her head might blow off. How dared he manhandle her in that casual, offhand manner? She was speechless, her eyes flashing with rage.

'Sit down.' Jake pushed her into one of the chairs which were positioned around the balcony. She tried to stand up almost immediately, but he pushed her back again, his face tightening as he controlled his temper. 'Sit down, and stay down!'

She gritted her teeth, recognising the futility of arguing with him. It was like trying to conduct an argument with an armoured tank. He would take absolutely no notice of her protests, riding roughshod over any feelings she might present to him.

She lowered her eyes, seething with impotent rage, and rubbed her wrist. There was an angry red mark on her skin where he had exerted pressure on her wrist.

'What happens now?' she asked tartly without looking up. 'Do you bring on the Spanish Inquisition?'

He towered over her, his face grim and unsmiling, his whole body taut with the threat of unleashed violence. 'Don't be clever, it doesn't suit you.'

Her eyes flickered upwards, gliding over the muscular legs, the lean waist and hips, the powerful chest, finally coming to rest on his face. 'What does suit me, I wonder?' she said with a sting in her voice. 'Being held up to ridicule and contempt perhaps? Is that how you see me?'

'Don't try to over-dramatise it.'

She laughed bitterly. 'Over-dramatise? I don't need to—it's melodramatic enough all on its own. I felt like a music-hall joke—married five hours and my husband already had his mistress in his bed!'

'That's not what happened,' he bit out. 'That's only what you think happened.'

'Oh, I'm blind as well as stupid now, am I?'

There was a short, very intense silence. Neither of them moved or spoke, and the silence hung between them like a thick black cloud.

Jake turned his head away from her, moving to lean his hands on the wall of the balcony, looking out over lamplit London. Laura eyed him uncertainly, tracing the lines of his face, the strong jaw, the straight, faintly arrogant nose.

London was spread out before them, hazy lights

glowing around famous buildings in the distance. She picked out Big Ben from the glittering array, its clock face glowing like a white sun, looking down on the Embankment which was hidden from their view. The night air was crisp and fresh, softened with a summer dew. Laura could see three of the bridges, their tiny lights illuminating the Thames, glittering and shining in the darkness. It was a magical, breathtaking scene, and she only wished she could have viewed it under different circumstances.

Jake looked at her over his shoulder and their eyes met. 'I can understand your feelings,' he said in a clipped, curt voice.

'Can you?' her face was cold. 'Can you really, Jake?'

His mouth tightened. 'Damn you . . .' He bit the words off without continuing, his hard-boned face taut with anger.

Laura stood up slowly. 'What did you expect? Sympathy and understanding? If you can't control your sex drive, you'll have to learn to expect difficulties when it gets in the way of other people's lives.'

He straightened, taking a step towards her. 'You're letting your parents' mistakes colour your attitudes towards marriage.'

'I don't need their mistakes to show me what a marriage can do to two people. You managed to show me quite adequately all on your own.'

His eyes blazed. 'I'm not your father. Just because he had a string of mistresses it doesn't mean that's automatically the way every marriage turns out.'

'Oh no?' she hissed, her face and tone bitter. 'What was that girl doing in your bed, then?'

His hands took her shoulders in a biting grip. 'You

were ripe for it,' he muttered between his teeth. 'You were just waiting for something to happen that would block out every chance we ever had.'

'Oh, it's my fault now, is it?' Laura laughed bitterly. 'You're blaming me for your own weakness.'

His teeth clamped together like a steel trap. 'You set yourself up as judge and jury. You put your little black cap on and condemned me without a fair trial.'

She struggled against the punishing hands which gripped her shoulders. 'Don't speak to me in metaphors!' she snapped, her fists pushing aimlessly against the hard wall of his chest. 'They aren't going to get you out of this one. You were in bed with another woman—I saw you with my own eyes. What defence could you possibly have? What greater piece of evidence than witnessing a disgusting little scene like that? I caught you redhanded, Jake. You *have* no defence.'

His face darkened, his eyes blazing with anger. The skin across those hard cheekbones tautened, showing white over the bone. 'You ask for trouble, don't you?' he growled, and his hands dug painfully into her flesh.

Laura's nose was level with the white silk of his shirt and she slowly raised her head to look at him.

'Don't threaten me,' she said unsteadily, seeing the menace in every line of his body.

A cruel smile touched his lips. 'Not quite so sure of yourself now, Laura?' he asked in a deep, smoky voice, and she shivered.

There was a short silence. Her eyes widened with a sudden upsurge of fear, her spine prickling with alarm. Her heart began to thud in a jerky rhythm, her throat dry and tight. She couldn't tear her eyes away from him. He mesmerised her, his body poised for violence, as though he was a dangerous jungle cat, waiting to spring.

'Let go of me!' she whispered through dry lips.

The grim face was carved out of granite. His eyes burned through her, and her heart thudded faster in panic and fear.

'Let go of me,' she repeated, her voice trembling slightly.

The air crackled with electricity. Her gaze focused on the strong hard mouth, her pulses pounding furiously in her ears, her whole body taking up the harsh, jerky rhythm.

She heard his swift intake of breath, and her eyes flashed to his, widening in alarm as she realised what she had done. She shrank away from him, her tongue darting out across her dry lips.

'No, please . . .' she whispered.

Jake pulled her against him, his head swooping down to claim her mouth in a slow, burning kiss. Heat flashed through her, weakening her limbs, filling them with a melting sensation which increased the thud of her heart until it crashed against her breastbone with terrifying intensity.

His hot mouth moved over her, his hands sliding sensuously up and down her back, caressing her hips, pressing her against the hard length of his body. The muscular thighs pressed against her own trembling thighs and she groaned, feeling the heat flood her cheeks until they burned.

'Laura,' he muttered thickly, his long fingers stroking her stomach. Her hands slid up over his shoulders in a groan of submission, tangling in the thick black hair which rested on his collar.

The kiss deepened, their hearts crashing against each other as they pressed together in a heat of desire.

Jake drew his head back to look down at her, the blue eyes glittering with a sexual intensity which brought her back to her senses. He had always been able to reach her with a touch of that sensuous mouth, control her, pacify her.

'Darling,' he muttered, focusing once more on her lips.

Not again, she thought wildly. He can't get away with it more than once. I can't let him. She broke away from him, breathing harshly. 'Why can't you leave me alone?' she whispered bitterly.

They stared at each other for a moment in total silence. Then Laura turned on her heels and ran out of the balcony and away from him, aware that those cruel blue eyes were stabbing at her every inch of the way.

The weekend passed in a daze of anxiety clouded with bitter memories. She stayed in her flat in constant fear, her ears pricked for the sound of a powerful engine, the click of his heels on the path heralding his arrival. Her relief was almost tangible when Jake showed no signs of turning up. By Sunday night her nerves were in shreds, her teeth locked together in a permanent jarring fear, her hands clenched into fists. She crawled into bed, falling asleep over a period of two hours as her limbs slowly began to unlock.

She went to work the next day on a cloud of hope. If Jake wanted to get in touch with her, he would have done so by now; he did not waste time when he wanted something. Laura was at work early, her face brooding and pensive. As there was no one else around at eight-thirty, she had nothing to do but sit and think. Mistake, she thought wryly as she felt her thoughts wander uncontrollably back to the past, and Jake.

She had first met him when she was working for a broadcasting company in the north of England. She had joined up with the London network, and had dotted around the country, working for a few months at a time in different studios.

Jake had been there to sign up an actress for his own company. Laura had been taking coffee and sandwiches to her boss, and was having difficulty with the door, balancing the tray in one precarious hand. She hadn't been aware of anyone behind her until a cool dark voice had spoken at her shoulder.

'Can I help?'

She had turned her head on a reflex movement to stare up into the most dazzling blue eyes she had ever seen, fringed with lashes which curled back sexily, resting on a hard tanned cheek.

He had leaned over, his powerful chest resting on her shoulder, and clicked open the door. But he hadn't moved away. They had stared at each other in silence for a moment, their faces close, almost touching. Then he had stepped back, allowing her to pass.

She had been aware of those unnerving blue eyes burning on her while she walked into the office, but she hadn't turned her head, frightened of what he might have been able to read in her eyes.

It was a week later when she was filing in her office and heard the door click open. She had slowly turned around, her spine prickling with awareness tinged with fear. Jake had leant against the door with lazy grace, watching her with those unnerving blue eyes.

'Have dinner with me,' was all he said.

Laura had been afraid to accept at first. She had been only nineteen, hardly old enough to be dating someone as sophisticated and experienced as Jake Ashton. But he hadn't taken no for an answer. He had pressed his invitation on her with a charming, heart-warming smile, and she had finally accepted.

They were engaged a month later. Laura saw him every night; dining with him, going to the theatre with him, the occasional night-club or party. She had been blissfully happy, secure in her love for him. And she had loved him. My God, she thought now, as she stared out of the window at the cold early morning, I really loved you, Jake.

Her lips twisted with wry bitterness. He obviously hadn't loved her as much as she had thought he had.

Her mind flitted back to the night they had got engaged. He had held her gently in his arms, his hands resting on her back. 'Trust me,' he had murmured in a husky voice against her lips, 'trust me, Laura. I'll never hurt you.'

She had rested her head against his broad shoulder with a sigh. 'I'm frightened, Jake. It's all happened too quickly, I can't seem to keep up with it. How do I know you'll always love me this much?'

He had drawn his head back then, to look down at her gravely. 'Laura, I can understand the way you feel. But I'm not your father, and you aren't your mother. We're too totally different people. I won't leave you—ever.'

She had smiled up at him, seeing the love in his eyes. 'I love you,' was all she could say, the rest of the words got caught up in a husky tangle of emotion.

Jake had bent his head with a groan, his mouth moving possessively over hers in a slow burning kiss, and she had surrendered to his kiss, pushing aside all fears and doubts. After all, he had asked her to trust him. What more could she do? She felt she owed him her trust, and she was happy to give it.

She shivered now, pulling her arms about herself. Perhaps that was all that had ever been between them, sexual attraction. No, she thought grimly, sexual attraction couldn't produce that much pain. Not in a million years.

When they had been married, she had floated on a wonderful cloud high above everyone else's heads. After the ceremony, Jake had taken her in his arms outside the church. The sunshine had spilled through the clouds, warming her face as he lifted her chin and bent to press his sensual mouth on hers.

'You're mine,' he had murmured as he drew away, and she had been filled with a luxurious happiness which bubbled up inside her as they slid into the car in each other's arms to drive to the reception.

But as the afternoon changed slowly into evening, Laura had been filled with fear at the thought of the coming night. She felt so small and frail next to Jake. She became nervy and jumpy as time wore on, and she noticed Jake watching her through thick lashes, his eyes reading her mind.

When they had gone to change for the honeymoon, he had stopped outside her room to speak to her for a moment. 'Don't look so worried, my darling,' he had admonished, stroking her cheek gently with one long finger, 'I shan't hurt you or rush you, I promise.'

She had taken a long time getting dressed for the

honeymoon journey. Her mother had helped her, fussing over her suit and make-up until they decided she was at last ready. Then Laura had wandered down to Jake's room, surprised that he wasn't ready before her.

Her heart had thumped with nerves as she knocked timidly on his door. There were muffled sounds from within, and she had pushed the door open, a curious frown on her face.

Her frown turned to a look of horror as her eyes swept over the frozen tableau in front of her. Jake, lying on the bed, his shirt off, the hard, muscled chest gleaming with a dark, silky tan. The beautiful girl next to him, her slender body encased in a loose, almost transparent chiffon dress.

Her eyes had darted from the girl's swollen lips, to the smudge of lipstick on Jake's cheek, his tousled hair. She had stared at him, pain written all over her face as her heart kicked agonisingly in her chest.

'Laura . . .' Jake had stood up, his face anxious, and came towards her, stretching out a bare, tanned arm.

But she had seen enough. She ran to her room, leaning over the basin as the sickness came and went in terrible waves, her eyes watering as she dimly heard his voice from what seemed like a great distance.

Her mother had been patting her on the shoulder, her voice worried, curious, enquiring. It had all seemed so painfully ridiculous as she looked up at her through a mist of tears and sickness, seeing her mother standing there, her lilac hat slightly askew, her teeth stained with lipstick as she bit into her lip with anxiety.

Then Jake had come into the room, trying to explain in clipped brief terms to her mother exactly what had happened. 'She's only just arrived back,' he had said, trying to reach Laura while her mother held him back, 'She didn't know about us, and she was hurt. I had to explain to her.'

And then her mother's incredulous voice, repeating, 'She? She?' as her eyes darted from Jake to Laura and a look of horror and disgust came over her face.

Laura had looked up then, bitterly. 'And what about me? Don't I count?' Her pain had been mirrored in her eyes. 'Don't you care if you hurt me?'

Her mother had become angry then, arguing with him, telling him to get out, while Jake's voice became thicker, filled with raw emotion, which Laura had taken to be anger. He had tried again and again to get to Laura, make her listen to him. But her mother had finally stopped him.

'Haven't you done enough?' she had asked in a tone filled with disgusted anger, and silence had fallen instantly. Jake had left the room quietly, telling them he would come back when they had both calmed down.

'They're all the same,' her mother had muttered bitterly, helping Laura to wash her face, and Laura had seen the bitterness in her mother's face and recognised it to be the same terrible anger which she felt. There was no way which she could ever wipe out that awful sickness she had felt as she had looked at Jake and that girl lying on the bed together on her wedding day.

Her mother had helped her home, sneaking out of the back exit together like a couple of thieves in the night, and it had only increased Laura's feeling of sickness and despair.

'You never have to see that man again,' her mother had told her as they drove home in the car. 'I wish I'd had the same warning when I married your father. I could have saved myself a lot of trouble and heartache if I'd only seen into his head at the start.'

Laura had stared out of the window, watching the streets flash past with painful clarity, taking her farther and farther away from Jake. All her dreams, she had thought at the time, and all her happiness had been wrapped up in that one man. Jake had held her heart in his hands, and he had crushed it without compunction.

Her mother had made her some tea while Laura stared into space, trying to cut through the numb icy feeling inside her. 'That's one thing my life with your father taught me, Laura,' her mother had told her gently, stroking her hair as she looked into her daughter's pain-filled eyes. 'Men need a lot of different women, but women need only one man. They can't help themselves, I suppose. They don't care who it is——' and her mother's lips had suddenly twisted with bitterness, 'don't care if it's your own sister.'

She had looked at her mother then, as she relived again and again in her mind that icy horror when she had walked into Jake's bedroom. The same replay was covered by a similar horror of long ago; her father and another woman. The numbness broke, and the most indescribable pain cut deep inside her like a knife. The tears started.

'That's right,' her mother had soothed, holding her as she rocked back and forth, 'cry it all out.'

'I'm dying,' Laura had thought, unable to describe it any other way. 'I'm dying.'

It had been about ten o'clock when the hammering on the door started. Laura had hidden in her room, unable to face Jake, and her mother had gone to the door, bristling with anger.

'Get out before I call the police!' Her mother's angry voice reached her ears, and she winced, shivering with fear as she heard Jake's angry voice arguing with her.

'Get out of my way!' she had heard him snarl as his footsteps came towards her bedroom door, and Laura had felt the shaking start.

Jake had burst in, slamming the door behind him, and she had shrunk from the burning anger in his eyes. Her mother had tried to get into the room after him, but he had forced her out, and eventually she had given up.

Jake had pleaded with Laura to listen to him, but she had been too bitterly hurt and disappointed. She hadn't been able to listen to one word he said. He had tried every method he could think of to get her to listen; soothing, pleading, shouting, and finally, physical violence.

His temper had snapped. He had snarled viciously at her, clamping one powerful arm around her, forcing her, struggling furiously, back across the bed. The strong, cruel hands had ripped her nightdress to shreds, inflicting bruises on her pale, shivering body.

She fought him tooth and nail, trying desperately to prevent the invasion of her body. But he was clever, experienced, and his hands had wrung a bitter response from her which took over from her anger and gave way to heated passion.

When he had released her, his heartbeat still echoing through her body, she had turned, disgusted and humiliated, on her side, sobbing with rage. Her response had appalled her, it had been so unexpected and intense that she was furious with herself.

He had turned her to face him, his eyes intense, his face grim. He had apologised, trying to explain what she had witnessed. But Laura wouldn't listen. She had jumped off the bed, pulling a dressing gown around herself, flinging bitter insults at him. She had said she felt dirty, cheap, and she had—she had felt brutally used and defiled.

Eventually Jake had left under a brooding cloud of anger, telling her he would return the next day, leaving her alone for the night to think things through. She had watched him go, a bitter, flaring anger in her eyes.

She had left the house the next morning, staying at various friends' houses over the next fortnight until she finally found a new place to live.

She had never seen him again since that day. For ten days after her flight he had repeatedly gone to her mother's, banging on the door, demanding Laura's new address. But her mother had refused point-blank to give him any clue. She had been through a similar experience with Laura's father, and she had no intention of allowing her daughter to suffer as she had suffered.

After a while Jake had got the message, and left them both alone. Laura had always been curiously irritated with him for giving up after only ten days. But then, she had told herself, what could she expect from a man who could be unfaithful on his wedding day?

So she had settled into her new life happily, and gradually the bitterness had faded, leaving her only a pattern of occasional sleepless nights when his dark, arrogant face crept into her dreams to disturb her.

Laura sighed now, staring out of the window. Why did the past always catch up with you eventually? She had dreaded their meeting for so long that now it had actually happened, it was something of a relief. But it was also a threat—a very big threat.

The door of the office opened, and Carly wandered in dressed in a loosely-belted silk dress, a lightweight silk jacket slung over her fine-boned shoulders with casual elegance.

She raised an eyebrow at Laura. 'What have we here?' she drawled, walking across the office to her own desk. 'An early bird? Caught anything yet?'

Laura chuckled. 'Only a particularly nasty cup of coffee.' She gestured towards the plastic cup on her desk.

Carly moved her shoulders gracefully, and the silk jacket slithered off into her hands. 'We must get a kettle and make our own. Meanwhile, I'll continue to poison my insides. Get me some, would you?'

Laura walked to the machine and got her some black coffee, handing it to her with a smile. 'Good weekend?' she asked politely.

Carly accepted the coffee with a languorous smile. 'Are you kidding?'

Laura chuckled, moving back to her desk, and Carly followed, perching elegantly on the edge of it.

'Speaking of the weekend,' she drawled, her mouth lifting at the corner, 'do we have any news from our man on the spot?'

'Man on the spot?'

'That's you, sweetie.'

Laura studied her with a puzzled frown, her head tilted to one side. 'Sorry, I think I must have missed something. Why am I the man on the spot?'

Carly sipped her coffee. 'You remember—exclusive one-hour interview with the delicious Mr Jake Ashton on Friday night.'

Laura felt the heat creeping into her cheeks. She had hoped Carly would let it pass, but she obviously had other ideas. Laura picked up some papers from the tray by her desk.

'Oh, that,' she said evasively, looking down at the work in her hands.

'Yes, that,' Carly drawled. She leant forward and took the papers from Laura, her cat-like eyes pinning her to her chair. 'Come on, tell Carly.'

Laura observed her, her face blank. 'Tell Carly what?'

Carly's eyebrows rose slowly. 'Interesting,' she murmured. 'Sudden memory loss. Or are you feeling suddenly mysterious this morning?'

'Not particularly,' she smiled. 'You're the one who's being mysterious. I really don't know what you're talking about.'

Carly's eyes narrowed into slits, and she studied her for several seconds in silence. Then she slid languorously off the desk. 'Okay. This is one scoop I keep my hands off, right?'

Laura bent her head. 'No scoop here, I'm afraid,' she muttered, picking up her work from the desk.

Carly wandered off, and the door opened once more. This time it was one of the other assistants in their department, and the office began buzzing as more staff filed in to begin work.

Laura worked steadily through the morning, breaking only for coffee now and then. She took time over her work before sending it down to Carly for a final check.

At twelve-thirty, she leaned back in her seat and stretched her arms. Carly caught her eye.

'Okay, sleepyhead, you can take your lunch now,' she drawled, looking at the slim gold watch around her fine-boned wrist. 'Back at one-thirty, though, or heads will roll.'

Laura grinned, standing up and picking her bag up just as the telephone began ringing again. She walked to the door.

'Laura!' Carly's voice caught her just as she was closing the door, and she put her head round it to look across the room. 'Telephone!' Carly waved the receiver at her.

Laura frowned, crossing the office. 'Who is it?'

Carly's red mouth curled. 'I don't know, but he sure as hell sounds sexy. Does the rest of him match up to his voice?'

Laura didn't reply, taking the receiver with a slightly uncertain hand. 'Hello?'

'Hello, Laura.' The deep, smoky voice sent a prickle of fear running down her spine.

She gripped the receiver. 'What do you want?'

He laughed softly. 'Do I have to spell it out?' Laura's lips tightened with the desire to smash the receiver down in its cradle and stop that insolent, taunting voice.

Out of the corner of her eye she could see Carly watching curiously. If she slammed the phone down, Carly wouldn't let her rest until she told her who had been on the other end of the line.

'Was there anything else?' she asked in a sweet,

honeyed voice which made it clear to Jake that she was not amused by his comment.

'Of course,' he murmured. There was a pause, and she waited silently for him to speak again. 'Have dinner with me.'

She was taken aback, a frown marring her brow. 'No,' she said after a moment. 'No, I won't.'

There was another pause. 'Lunch, then?'

Laura glanced at Carly anxiously, and the other girl seemed to get the message. She stood up with a wry smile and wandered over to speak to one of the other assistants.

Laura turned back to the phone. 'I'm sorry, I can't.'

Jake spoke in a clipped, angry voice. 'Don't try to avoid me, Laura. I'll get to you somehow.'

His voice made her tense involuntarily, her muscles clutching each other. She believed him. He would go to great lengths to get what he wanted, and if she tried to stand in his way he would rip her apart.

'Well?' His voice sniped at her.

Her heart was beating fast, her palms growing wet as she clutched the telephone, forcing her voice to sound strong. 'No, Jake. I'm sorry, but the answer is no.'

She heard his voice, biting out a muffled oath. Slowly she put the receiver back in its cradle, staring at it blankly. He knew where she worked, it would only be a matter of time before he found out her address. She had two days, perhaps three at the most. He wouldn't contact her again. He would keep her hanging on a thread. He would let her sweat it out.

Bastard, she thought, he's playing games with me.

CHAPTER THREE

LAURA sat in her flat later that evening, curled up in a chair, trying to read a book. She flicked through the pages restlessly, the words blurring before her eyes. She put it down on the table with a disgusted thud. It was like trying to read Chinese; she couldn't seem to take any of it in. Her concentration level was falling below zero.

The doorbell rang, and Laura looked up, sitting quite still for a moment. It couldn't be Jake, could it? She shook her head, frowning. It was probably one of the girls upstairs. They were both nurses, and came off duty at the same time, thus making it impossible for them to pick up milk on the way home from work. They were always dropping in on Laura, endearing smiles at the ready as they borrowed milk and sugar in vast quantities.

She opened the door. It was Jake, and Laura whitened as she looked up into his dark, arrogant face. She was motionless for a split second, her throat drying up, her heart moving on a wild surge of panic inside her.

Then she moved, but not fast enough. He kicked the door back open even as she was shutting it in his face. Laura fell against the wall, her eyes wide with sudden fear.

He slammed the door and moved farther into the flat with an air of menace. 'Don't ever do that again,

Laura,' he said, his mouth biting out the words, 'or I'll break your neck.'

She shivered. He looked dangerous, his face grim and unsmiling, the skin taut across his cheekbones, and Laura stared at him in dismay. 'You left me no choice,' she told him, her voice unsteady.

'What the hell does that mean?' he demanded.

She ran her tongue nervously over her lips. The blue eyes followed the little movement intensely, and she coloured, looking away from him. 'I told you this morning—I don't want to see you.' She looked back at him. 'But you took no notice. What do you expect me to do?' Her voice was husky. 'I had to get the message across somehow.'

There was a sudden flare of anger in his eyes. 'I don't like having doors slammed in my face,' he bit out. Then he took a deep breath, raking a hand through his thick black hair.

Laura didn't reply. She didn't really see that there was much point in trying to explain to him that she seriously did not want to see him. It hurt every time she looked upon that harsh, powerful face. He obviously thought otherwise, though, and there was very little she could do about that except try to avoid him whenever possible.

He was watching her intensely. 'Have dinner with me.'

She shook her head sadly. 'No, Jake.'

He didn't speak for a moment, and she could see that he was weighing up his words before he spoke, his body motionless. He shoved his hands into his pockets. 'Why?' The monosyllable was uttered in a curt, clipped tone.

She sighed. 'I've already told you, Jake, I just don't want to see you again.'

The hard mouth firmed into a straight, angry line. 'Tell me why,' he asked tightly. 'Give me one good reason.'

Laura sighed again, looking down at her hands. There were so many good reasons she could have given him, but she knew he wouldn't accept any of them. 'I don't think we have anything more to say to each other.' She paused, waiting for his reply, but when he was silent, she looked up again. 'I'm sorry, Jake.'

He watched her in silence for a moment, as though an inner conflict was taking place, reason fighting with anger. 'Get your coat,' he said eventually. 'I'm taking you to dinner.'

She stared at him. Was he deaf? 'You can really take a hint, can't you?'

Jake remained unmoved, his face carved out of granite.

He wasn't deaf, he was just plain obstinate. He refused to bow to her wishes; his arrogance and self-assurance would never allow him to give way to the words of a woman. 'Sarcasm is wasted on you, isn't it?' Her voice held a sting. 'It's too subtle. I can see I'm going to have to try the direct approach: Get out of my life and stay out.'

His eyes pinned her against the wall. 'Get your coat,' he repeated tightly.

Laura backed away, imperceptibly, suddenly frightened by the cruel violence which shone through in his eyes. Then she took a deep breath and stood her ground. If she continued to give way to this man, her life would tumble in ruins about her feet, leaving her alone once more to pick up the pieces and try to fit them together.

His gaze flicked over her face as though he could read the rebellion inside her, then he smiled coldly. 'Very well, if you'd prefer to stay here, that's what we'll do.'

Her lips tightened with irritation. He was backing her into a corner, and he knew it. She didn't want to stay here alone in her flat with him—it would be risking too much, and she wasn't prepared to risk anything. She sighed. There was only one way out.

'Very well,' she said on a deep sigh. 'Wait a minute, I'll get my coat.' She went into her bedroom, feeling tense and nervous. Why did Jake have to keep pursuing her so relentlessly when she had made it more than clear that she wasn't interested?

She picked up her coat from the chair by her bed, and slung the lightweight cotton over her shoulders. Her eyes wandered to the mirror in the wardrobe, glancing down over her thin summer dress. She had worn it to work that day, but she didn't see why she should have to change it. If she wasn't good enough for Jake like this, she thought irritably, he would just have to lump it.

She went back into the hall to find him waiting patiently for her by the open door. She gave him a look of irritation as she walked past him out into the warm summer evening. Jake walked beside her to the long silver limousine which waited silently by the kerb.

Laura slid into the luxurious seat of the car while Jake held the door open for her. Her eyes followed him as he strode round to his side of the car. The wind blew a strand of the thick black hair softly, and he raked it back down with one hand as he opened the door and slid into the seat beside her.

She turned to him with an expression of resentment. 'Have you booked a table?' she asked.

He slid the key into the ignition with one long, sinewy hand. 'Yes.' His reply was clipped and curt.

Her lips compressed into an angry line. 'Sure of yourself, aren't you?' she snapped before she could stop herself, but Jake merely smiled and did not reply.

They pulled smoothly away from the kerb. Laura turned her head to gaze out of the window. London was bathed in a half-light as dusk fell over the city. The street lamps still glowed red as they lit up the warm summer evening with a dull glow. A handful of stray commuters picked their way along the street from the tube station, their faces tired and drawn as they made their way home, carrying briefcases, their heads bent. A group of children played in the street, their gamin faces happy, lit up with laughter as they rode around on bicycles, some of them playing around a lamp-post, a long skipping rope tied around its middle.

Laura found herself wondering why Jake had come to see her tonight. How had he found her address? She shrugged mentally. He had probably asked Rupert at some stage after ringing her that morning. Rupert was hardly likely to refuse to give it to him—Jake was a powerful man; he always got what he wanted in the end. Even me, she thought bitterly, turning her head to look at him once more.

The darkness hid his face in shadows, silhouetted briefly as they passed a lamp-post, lighting it up, showing her the strong, clean-shaven jaw, the arrogant, assertive bone-structure which made the deep strength of his face so devastatingly powerful.

'Where are you taking me?' she asked him in a subdued voice.

He turned cold eyes on her, a glimmer of amusement on his face. 'Wait and see,' was all he said.

She settled back resentfully in her seat. Why did he have to be so mysterious? She was going to find out sooner or later, so why not tell her now? She definitely preferred the idea of sooner rather than later.

They pulled up outside a large, glittering hotel, and Laura's eyes strayed to the huge, lit-up building. A doorman stood outside, his liveried uniform lending an air of authority to his otherwise less than imposing stature.

Laura frowned. Where was the restaurant? She looked up and down the street in search of it, but all there was to be seen in the street was the hotel. She turned to look at Jake, but he had got out of the car and was striding round to her side to let her out.

'Where's the restaurant?' she asked, eyeing him warily as he took her arm in a possessive grip.

'Inside the hotel,' he told her blandly, leading her over to the threshold. The doorman tilted his cap and said, 'Good evening', as they walked past him, but Laura barely noticed him. Her eyes were darting around the ground floor of the hotel, seeking out the restaurant. She pulled back from Jake as he led her across the foyer towards the lifts.

'Where are we going?' she asked, the first stirrings of panic beginning inside her.

He smiled briefly. 'The restaurant is on another floor.'

Laura frowned. There was something funny going on here. Her eyes alighted on a sign in the corner of the foyer which pointed out the restaurant—on the ground floor. She pulled her arm out of his grasp with an angry exclamation.

'You must think I'm stupid!' Her eyes flashed angrily. 'I'm not going up there with you.'

The lift doors slid open, people stepping out and around Jake and Laura, their faces holding the bland, uninterested expressions of the wealthy. Jake took her arm and pulled her inside the lift, holding her still against his hard body as she struggled.

'I'd like to see how you're going to stop me,' he murmured against her ear as the lift doors slid shut once more.

Laura watched in impotence as Jake pressed the button marked six. The red numbers above the door of the lift began to mark their ascent as the lift moved upwards smoothly.

She turned to Jake with an expression of burning hatred. 'Why are you doing this?' she asked between her teeth. 'Can't you get it through your head that I don't want to see you any more?'

Jake watched her for a second in silence, his face harsh and forbidding, then a cruel smile flickered across the dark features. 'I've told you before. I want to speak to you.'

'Well, I don't want to speak to you. We have nothing to say to each other.' Laura stood against the wall of the lift, keeping her distance as much as possible from him.

The blue eyes narrowed on her. 'You're wrong,' he said abruptly. 'We have too much to say to each other. Running away won't change that, it'll only postpone it.'

The doors slid open. Laura stared at him for a moment, uncertain as to her best course of action. The hard blue eyes stared back, and she slowly turned to walk out of the lift and into the large hallway which she found herself in.

Jake followed her, opening a door on her right and leading her inside with one strong hand on her arm. The room in which she stood was large, at least thirty feet long, decorated in shades of ivory and gold. Pictures lined the walls, making it seem more of a home than a hotel room.

'Is this your suite?' she asked as he closed the door behind them.

Jake nodded, standing next to her, sliding both hands into the pockets of his superbly cut black trousers.

Laura's eyes travelled over the length of the beautiful room, then stopped as she saw the three doors leading off to the left. She turned to Jake. 'You seem to be writing the script around here,' she said, her voice rich with irritation. 'What happens next? Exit stage left to the bedroom?'

He raised one jet black brow, a smile lifting the corners of his hard mouth. 'I thought I was the one with an obsession about sex! It must be catching.'

Laura gritted her teeth. She had asked for that one. She searched around for a really crushing reply.

'No comeback, Laura?' His voice was mocking. 'You must be losing your touch.'

'Funny!' she snapped. 'I'm afraid my sparkling wit deserts me when I've been manhandled half-way across London.'

He studied her for a moment, his black head tilted to one side. 'I must try it more often. If that's the effect it has, then it's obviously worthwhile.'

She drew a deep breath. 'I shouldn't,' she warned with a blistering smile. 'The idea doesn't appeal, somehow.'

He laughed softly under his breath. 'In that case, you'd better learn to do as you're told.'

His arrogance took her breath away. She stared at him, her eyes hating him. 'Is that just another way of telling me you're a selfish bastard, Jake?'

'Oh, I wouldn't say I was selfish,' he murmured, taking a step towards her. He towered over her, his eyes roving insolently over her body, his face only a few inches from her own, then he smiled. 'But I would say that I know what I want.' His lips brushed hers softly as his black head came towards her. 'And I know how to get it.' His voice was throaty as he finished, his lips touching hers again in a burning, teasing kiss.

Laura's heart stopped fractionally as she gazed into his hard-boned face, her pulses beginning to thud in the same rhythm. He was so close. She swallowed on a dry throat.

Jake's hands went to her shoulders, slipping the lightweight coat over her shoulders, and her hands fluttered up to catch at the coat. 'Don't . . .' she said breathlessly as it slid from her shoulders.

His eyes burned on her, and Laura stared up into them as though she were hypnotised.

The knock at the door shocked her out of her

thoughts. Jake raised his well-shaped black head. 'Come in,' he called crisply.

The door opened and a tall, stately man entered. He looked over the top of his long Roman nose at them with a bland expression. 'Good evening, sir, madame,' said the man in crisp, middle-class tones. 'They rang to let us known you had arrived.'

Jake nodded. 'Thank you, Travers. We'll be ready to eat any time.'

Travers adjusted his cuffs. 'Very good, sir. Will there be anything else?'

'No, that will be all.'

Travers nodded his bald head and left the room with a swish as he closed the door behind him.

Jake looked down at Laura in silence for a moment, then he turned and walked further into the room. 'Sit down,' he told her as he walked over to what appeared to be a drinks cabinet.

Laura sighed with relief as she walked over to the armchair. Thank God for Travers, she thought, sitting down in the large leather armchair. If he hadn't come in when he had, she knew she would not have been able to deal with Jake.

He still had the power to make her heart beat just a little too fast. He could still arouse her as easily as he had been able to a year ago. She would have to guard against that. Her hatred for him should have proved an effective barrier against his brand of sexuality—but obviously it wasn't.

Laura shivered, a peculiar frisson of alarm running down her spine. If she let him get too close, he would smash the fences she had put up to protect herself, he would tear down the barriers and break her into tiny pieces. She knew she wouldn't come through it again. She had been hurt too much. She just wasn't strong enough to rebuild her world a second time.

One can't avoid pain and disappointment, but one can look out for people and situations that will cause it—and avoid them.

'What do you want?' Jake asked her.

She looked up blankly. 'Oh, Martini, please,' she said in a dull voice. She hoped he wouldn't keep her here long. The sooner she got away from him, the better.

Her eyes strayed over the walls, seeing all the different paintings which hung there. The suite was beautifully decorated, expensive but not over-opulent.

An icy pain sliced through her as her eyes fell on one of the paintings. She couldn't take her eyes from it. 'I see you still have *The Swan of Eden*,' she said in a quiet voice.

Jake stood in front of her and handed her the long slim glass, looking down at her through heavy-lidded eyes. 'Yes. I thought I'd keep it in London.'

Her heart felt cold as she looked at the beautiful blues and golds of the painting, the slender young couple who stood in the protective shade of the huge white swan, the moonlight glittering magically over the water near them.

Laura swallowed, her hand clutching her glass tightly. Jake had bought it for her two weeks before their wedding. It was to have hung in their bedroom. *The Swan of Eden*: it should have been a part of their paradise. Laura laughed bitterly inside; she had thought she was entering paradise, but she had entered a nightmare.

Jake sat down opposite her, still watching her through those heavy lids, and Laura avoided his eyes. She raised the glass to her lips with an unsteady hand, feeling the cool liquid slide refreshingly over her dry throat. Her nerves began to tighten as she felt the heavy silence fall over them.

Laura began to hear the clock in the corner tick, counting the seconds relentlessly as the silence grew into a disturbing black cloud which hung over them with an air of menace.

There was a knock at the door, and Jake slowly raised his head, his eyes leaving her reluctantly. Laura was glad of the intrusion. An overwhelming relief flooded through her.

'Come in!' Jake called.

Travers entered with a swish. He adjusted his cuffs, observing them steadily over the end of his Roman nose. 'Dinner,' he announced blandly, 'is served.'

Jake nodded, then he looked back at Laura. 'Shall we go in?' His voice was soft.

Laura stood up slowly, putting her glass on the table in front of her with a little crash. She followed him into the large dining room where Travers waited discreetly with silver trays laden with food.

The dinner was beautifully prepared and laid out. Under normal circumstances, Laura would have enjoyed herself. But these were not normal circumstances. Jake made her feel uncomfortable, on edge.

She knew he had brought her here for a reason—Jake never did anything without a reason. He didn't waste any more time than he thought necessary. Laura knew him well enough to realise that he was saving something for her until the end of the evening.

They stayed on neutral subjects throughout the meal. Jake told her some amusing stories about the things that happened at his television studios. Laura did her best to smile and behave naturally. But something was stopping her.

She was grateful when they moved back into the drawing room for coffee. Jake somehow manoeuvred her into sitting next to him on the couch, and she found her nerves stretched to breaking point by the effect of his close proximity.

She searched around for something to say to him, her eyes darting aimlessly around the room. Then a thought struck her. She hadn't known he had a suite in London. Last time she had known him, he had always taken hotel rooms or stayed with friends. Had he had this place all the time—somewhere to bring his other women?

She turned to him with suspicious eyes. 'How long have you had this place?' she asked, trying to keep her voice as light and casual as she possibly could.

He raised one brow. 'Six months. So you can get that idea right out of your head.'

She blushed, turning her head away. He was too shrewd, too clever. She looked down at the coffee cup in her hands, chewing on the inside of her lip.

Jake stood up. 'Do you want a liqueur?' he asked in that deep rich voice, and Laura shook her head.

'No, thanks, I'll just stick to coffee,' she said quietly.

Jake went to the smooth oak cabinet, taking out a bottle and pouring himself some brandy. He moved back to the couch and sat down, stretching his long legs before him.

'So,' he asked casually, 'how long have you been with *Style* magazine?'

Laura pursed her lips for a moment in silence, then she said in a controlled voice, 'Don't tell me you don't know the answer to that one, Jake.'

He shrugged broad shoulders. 'I was merely trying to make polite conversation. However, you seem to be looking for an argument.'

Laura put her cup down on the table with a distinct crash. 'I don't know exactly why you brought me here, Jake, but I do know you did it for a reason.' She smiled bitterly. 'You never do anything without a reason, do you?'

'True,' he conceded, his black head tilted to one side as he watched her, 'but I thought you might prefer to stay on neutral subjects for a while.'

Did he think she was completely stupid? She surveyed him with angry green eyes. 'This is hardly what I would call a neutral subject. How long have you known where I was and who I worked for?'

There was a short pause, then he said, 'I've always known.'

She hadn't expected that, and something cold clutched at her heart as she stared at him in silence. It hurt to think that he had always known where to find her but had never bothered. I should have known, she thought blankly, I should have had more sense. His interest had only been renewed by their chance meeting in the nightclub. He had never intended to come back for her.

'I had a report on my desk a week after I got back to the States.' His voice broke into her thoughts.

Her head swung round. 'The States? But what were

you doing there?' She paused, her mind working quickly, then her lips tightened, her green eyes filled with bitterness. 'Oh, don't tell me, let me guess. Business before pleasure. You couldn't let a little thing like your wife leaving you get in the way of the Network.'

The blue eyes held hers coldly. 'I went back to New York because my brother had been killed.'

Laura fell silent, her eyes widening in amazement. He had to be joking. If Tom had been killed, she would have read about it.

'There was a big pile-up on Fifth Avenue. Tom was heading for the office, and he couldn't avoid it. A lot of people were injured.' He shrugged broad shoulders. 'Tom was killed.'

Laura swallowed on a dry throat, her eyes pained. She didn't know what to say. She had liked Tom, and to say that she was sorry seemed somehow inadequate, but it was all that she could say. 'I'm sorry,' she murmured quietly, 'I didn't know.'

'No,' he said sardonically, his eyes mocking as he studied her, 'you just jumped to conclusions as usual.'

That wasn't fair. She had liked Tom. She had only met him once, at their wedding. She had expected some opposition by marrying Jake—after all, he was a very powerful man. But Tom had been cheerful, bright, talkative, funny—he had welcomed her into the family with open arms, and she had been very grateful to him. It seemed incredible to think that he had been dead for a year without her ever having an inkling of it.

'After the funeral,' Jake continued, drawing on his cigar and regarding her through the silver-blue smoke with heavy-lidded eyes, 'there was an emergency conference called—shares dropped the minute the news got out, and I had to calm everyone down. By the time everything was cleared up, I knew it would be too late.'

Laura tilted her head to one side. 'Too late?' she queried. 'Too late for what?'

Jake studied her for a moment in silence, then he sat down slowly next to her, his face unreadable. 'Too late to come back,' he said softly. He raked a hand through his hair and glanced at her. 'I knew the bitterness would have had too much time to settle in, and I knew I would have a hell of a job trying to cut it out.'

Laura's eyes flared at that. 'Bitterness?' she echoed. 'What the hell do you know about it? Did you expect me to be happy?'

There was a fleeting expression of some emotion which Laura found difficult to grasp on Jake's face. He took her hand in a gentle movement, his eyes holding hers. 'I can understand how you felt,' he said in a soft voice.

She snatched her hand back angrily. 'Don't patronise me! How can you possibly understand how it felt?'

He stared at her, taken aback for a moment. Laura thought he was about to say something, but he fell silent instead, turning his head away from her. Her eyes strayed to his hands, which were clenched into fists, the whites of his knuckles showing through.

Laura shivered, feeling her courage slipping away like sand between her fingers. She could see he was angry—very angry. He was so unpredictable, his temper so volatile that she could never be sure when he was about to blow up.

She stood up, refusing to back down at this late

stage. Jake was the one man who could make her feel so threatened, so small and helpless. Every time he was near, all her strength and independence just flew out of the window.

'I think I'd better go,' she said, her voice slightly unsteady, her hands clenched into fists in an effort to calm herself.

He towered over her with an air of menace which made the hair on the back of her neck prickle. 'Sit down. You're not leaving.'

'That,' she retorted, 'is what you think.'

'You're not going anywhere, my darling,' he drawled in an icy voice. 'I don't give up that easily.'

He considered her from beneath heavy lids, his face grim and unsmiling. Then a cruel smile flickered across the dark features. 'I thought you knew me better than that,' he drawled mockingly. 'You should know by now that I never give up on something that is mine.'

Her eyes flared. 'What you mean is,' she snapped between tight lips, 'that you think you can come back after a year and expect me to drop everything and come running!'

He took another step towards her, making her feel small and insignificant beside his obvious strength. Her nose was level with the silk of his waistcoat, and she raised her head to look at him.

Jake smiled down at her coldly. 'You're mine,' he told her, 'I never let go of something that belongs to me.'

Her hands trembled. 'I don't belong to anyone but myself,' she said angrily. 'I married you because I loved you. Love is a gift, not a possession. You chose to throw away what I gave you. Well, it's not yours to take any more, Jake—you had your chance and you blew it.'

Dark angry colour invaded his face, his nostrils flaring white against his cheeks. 'You stubborn little bitch!' he bit out. 'You're so twisted up inside you can't see any man in any way except by linking him up with your past. You're still putting me in the same category as your father.'

That hurt. Her head came back on a snap of anger, her face whitening visibly at his words. He knew how much that statement would hurt her. He knew how she hated to talk about her father to anyone.

'You damned well belong there!' she said hoarsely. 'You both come out of the same mould.'

He gripped her shoulders. 'I'm not spending the rest of my life paying through the nose for other people's mistakes!' he snarled.

'Stop trying to sidestep by hiding behind my father!' Her voice trembled with the force of her anger. 'You're paying for your own mistakes. If you can't keep your hands off other women for longer than a few hours, that's your problem, not mine.' Her palms were damp, her heart beating convulsively against her breastbone. 'Now, will you let me get the hell out of here!'

His mouth clamped shut like a steel trap, his hands snaking out to take her wrists, pinning her arms behind her back as he pushed her, struggling, back until she was against the wall. 'I've told you,' he said cruelly, 'you're not going anywhere.'

Laura struggled against his effortless strength. 'Don't touch me!' she flung.

Jake smiled. 'That isn't what you used to say to me, my sweet.'

Her face held bitter distaste as she stared at him, her eyes hating him. 'You bastard, there's never anything else on your mind, is there?'

His smile grew savage. 'Not when I'm around you,' he said unpleasantly, his gaze searing on her flesh as it roved over her body. 'You're so exquisitely put together.'

She was breathing hard, trying to force down the shock-waves of sexual arousal which were flooding through her. 'I hate you!' she flung, knowing that she mustn't give in and let him win at this stage. 'I hate you to touch me!'

His hands tightened and she winced in pain. He smiled unpleasantly down at her. 'Isn't that tough?' he drawled icily. 'Isn't that just too bad?'

Her eyes widened and she shrank against the wall as his black head swooped down. 'Please, Jake,' she whispered, 'please don't. Let me go!' Her voice throbbed with sick panic.

His mouth clamped down on hers, forcing her lips apart back against her teeth until she tasted the salty flow of blood on her tongue. His hands pulled her roughly towards him, holding her so tightly she thought he might crush her.

She tried to twist her face away, but his hands came up, clamping her head in position, the long fingers biting into her cheeks as he held her. She moaned in protest.

Jake raised his head to look down at her with fevered eyes. 'Stop fighting me, Laura,' he muttered thickly.

Her heart stopped at the thick, slurred tone, then crashed back into life in harsh, disturbed movements.

His hot mouth moved against hers, his hands sliding

sensuously down her back, caressing her hips, stroking her skin through the thin summer dress. She trembled as she felt the hard thighs slide against hers.

A heated, molten excitement raced through her, and her hands slid over his shoulders, her fingers tangling in his thick black hair. She groaned in helpless response.

His mouth moved against hers with a heated sensuality, drawing a honeyed excitement into the slow, drugging kiss. The long fingers moved to stroke the flat planes of her stomach, and she arched her soft, feminine body against him.

Her strong sexuality fought against her common sense and won the battle hands down. Her mind and body were drowning in the long-forgotten sensations. Deep in the pit of her stomach, she felt the addictive, heated excitement melt her limbs.

Jake groaned from deep in the back of his throat as the kiss deepened, and Laura's eyelids fluttered open at the sound.

She saw the strong, powerful face in the grip of a heated sensuality, his eyes closed, his black brows drawn together in pleasure as he kissed her expertly. In that moment, he had lost. She hated him even more because he thought he had her in the palm of his hand. He thought he had won.

Not again, Jake, she thought bitterly, not this time, not with me. She pulled away jerkily.

His lids opened slowly, the thick black lashes curling back sexily as they rested on his tanned cheek. 'What is it, darling?' he asked in a husky murmur.

She forced a tight smile to her face. 'Very nice, Jake. But it's not going to work.'

He frowned. 'Laura. . . .'

'Seduction is not going to work,' she interrupted. She lifted her head in an unconscious gesture of defiance, the light shining on her head, picking out threads of copper in her red-gold hair. 'Not this time, not on me. In fact, it only goes to prove that I've been right about you all along. Your one main interest is sex, and you'll do anything to get it!'

His mouth firmed into an angry line. 'Don't be so bloody stupid! You know damned well that wasn't the idea. I kissed you because I wanted you—not because of some complicated strategy, and not because of some psychological defect.'

Laura bit her lip. 'Nevertheless, it won't get you anywhere.'

He caught her chin with one long sinewy hand and thrust her head back, tilting it towards him. The shrewd blue eyes focussed on her and a smile touched the sensual mouth.

'Are you telling me you didn't enjoy it?' he drawled mockingly, his steady gaze picking out the lingering signs of desire which were written all over her face.

'I hated it!' she lied, refusing to admit her own weakness.

He gave a harsh crack of laughter. 'You goddamned liar! You were with me all the way.'

Laura felt the colour seep into her cheeks, anger rising inside her for this bitter humilition. Why did he have to keep hurting her? Why couldn't he just leave her alone?

'Don't bet on it, Jake,' she snapped, breaking away from him, her eyes blazing. 'I don't want to be with you ever again!'

She turned, running blindly to the lift, slamming the door behind her and jamming her hand on the call button. She was breathing deeply, her eyes closed momentarily. She knew he would come after her, of course. But she wasn't going to let him stop her—not this time.

The door burst open seconds after she had left the room, and Jake came up behind her, whirling her around to face him.

'Where the hell do you think you're going?' he demanded tightly.

She swallowed, dragging up the last of her courage. 'I'm going home, Jake,' she told him. 'I don't want to stay here any longer.'

She thought she saw a fleeting expression of an emotion she couldn't quite grasp cross Jake's face. But then it was gone, and the mask slipped back into place.

'Laura,' his voice was soft, his brows drawn together in a frown as he studied her. 'Stay a little while longer. I still want to speak to you.'

The lift doors slid open as though in slow motion and Laura forced herself to step calmly inside them. Something was calling her back. Was it the urgency in his voice? The expression in his eyes?

'No, Jake,' she shook her head, her heart thumping out a slow, painful rhythm. 'It's all been said before.'

The lift doors slid shut, and the last thing she saw was his face, clouded once again by that expression, that emotion which she couldn't, wouldn't identify.

She sagged against the wall, feeling the strength leave her body. She felt weak, drained. It had been so hard, walking away from him, when she knew that deep down, she wanted to be with him. But she wasn't going to let herself in for more of the same. Only a fool would do that.

The night air was crisp and cool as she left the hotel, and Laura shivered, drawing her coat around herself. She glanced up at the top floor of the hotel, searching for Jake's room.

A curtain was drawn back, and a dark figure stood at a window high above her. She stared up at him, feeling the pain begin again. But it was too late, she told herself. Besides, that couldn't be Jake, looking out, watching her leave.

She turned her head away with sadness, and walked down to the main street. She would be able to get a taxi there, get home, and go to sleep. Forget about this disastrous evening.

Inside the hotel, Jake let the curtain fall back into place.

CHAPTER FOUR

In the week that followed their evening together, Laura found herself losing more and more sleep. She would lie awake at nights, watching the red glow of her clock, thinking endlessly of Jake. Her work began to suffer. She couldn't concentrate at the office; her mind was constantly on Jake and all that had been said between them.

His remarks about her father had hurt her, as he had known they would. She preferred to forget that part of her life, but it sprang up in her mind now, bringing painful memories to the foreground.

Her parents had been married young, at eighteen. They had been forced into an early marriage by her mother's pregnancy. She had been carrying Laura on her wedding day, and Laura had arrived six months later. Although they had loved each other deeply to start with, her parents had been unable to cope with the burden of responsibility thrust on them at such an early age, and things had started to go wrong.

Stewart Hadleigh, Laura's father, had tried his best, but had eventually turned his back on the demands a family of his own was making on him. His wife, Amanda, had been left to carry the greater part of their responsibilities. At first, she had done so happily, accepting Stewart's immaturity and inability to give up his freedom. But when she found out that he had been seeking pleasure elsewhere, she became bitterly angry. Stewart had pleaded with her to forgive him. A temporary lapse, he had told her, that was all; he had never been able to resist a pretty face.

So Amanda had accepted him back into the family unit, believing his story, and hoping he would settle down one day. But Stewart carried on living in his own dream world, escaping from his burden by spending his time with other women.

By the time Laura was ten, her father had a string of mistresses—girls he had met at the office, women he had known since his marriage to Amanda: in fact, anyone who pleased his eye turned his head, and made his life more pleasurable.

Amanda Hadleigh had to accept her husband's inability to settle down with one woman. She needed his financial support in order to keep the home going, she believed that Laura needed a father, and held on firmly, like a drowning woman, to the belief that one day he might settle down for good.

Her life was tinged with bitterness, and she fought to keep it from surfacing near Laura, but children are very sensitive to the moods of those around them, and Laura had a pretty good idea of the state of her parents' marriage.

Laura tried permanently to cheer her mother up when she swung from hope to bitter, helpless depression. She would keep a smile pinned firmly to her face, trying to make her mother see that everything was going to be all right. But it was too late. The die was cast.

The last straw came one morning when her mother, anxious to keep a happy atmosphere in the home, decided to take Laura out for the day. They took the tube into town to see the Tower of London. Laura and her mother had been determined to enjoy themselves, their optimism both brave and hopeless when Stewart was still continuing to stay away for days at a time, coming home sheepishly with flowers and promises to change his ways.

It was as they were crossing Tower Hill that they saw them—Stewart walking along arm in arm with another woman. He had stopped to kiss her in full view of Amanda and Laura, and Laura had felt her mother stiffen, recoiling as if from a blow. Then as she was clinging to her mother's hand, she had looked hard at the woman her father was kissing.

She had stared, in childish wonder, at her aunt Jennifer. Why was her father kissing her mother's sister in that funny way? she had thought. Amanda had turned on her heel, her face set with pain and anger, and had marched back to the tube station, dragging a confused and hurt Laura behind her.

She heard them arguing bitterly in the kitchen two nights later. She had sat on the stairs, her hands twisting in silent agony, crying silently as she prayed for them to stop.

She had never seen her father again. He had slammed out of the door and out of their lives, ignoring her high-pitched cries for him to come back, and Laura had never been able to completely trust a man again.

She sighed now, as she gazed blankly out of the window at the streets which lay beneath the office. Why did the past never let you go? It always hung on to you with painful fingers. She would never be able to forget her father, and she knew she could never forgive Jake's betrayal. It had cut too deeply.

She looked around the office, seeing the busy hum of life as people went on with their work while her life was falling apart at the seams. She sighed. She was getting morbid.

She stood up and walked over to the coffee machine in the corner. She still couldn't believe that Jake had actually been unfaithful to her on her wedding day. Her lips tightened in bitter resignation. It had happened all right; she had seen it with her own eyes.

She turned her head slightly as she heard someone come up behind her.

'Hello there,' drawled Carly, lounging elegantly against the machine, jingling some coppers in her hand. 'You finished?' she gestured towards the machine.

Laura nodded, taking her cup and standing back. 'Go ahead.'

'Thanks.' Carly put the coins in and pressed the buttons. 'How much more of that stuff are you going to drink?' She eyed the cup in Laura's hands. 'You'll catch some horrible disease if you aren't careful. That stuff's lethal in large doses.' She smiled languorously. 'Like men!'

Laura grinned, shrugging. 'Keeps me awake.'

Carly raised an eyebrow, her red mouth curling at the corners. 'Men, or the coffee?'

Laura laughed. 'The coffee.'

Carly shrugged slim shoulders, the silk shirt she wore rippling with the movement. 'Each to his own,' she drawled, eyeing her with amusement. 'I prefer a man to keep me awake personally,' she told Laura, flashing a wicked grin.

Laura shook her head. 'Really, Carly, you should be censored!' She strolled over to her own desk, and Carly followed, perching on the edge of her desk.

She studied Laura with sharp hazel eyes. 'What's up with you, Laura? You've been way off balance for the last week. I thought it'd clear up over the weekend,' she smiled, her perfectly plucked brows rising, 'but here we are, Monday morning, and you're still ten fathoms under. Why?'

Laura looked away from her. 'Just feeling a bit off lately, that's all,' she muttered, her hands fiddling restlessly with a pile of papers in front of her.

Carly's expression was wry. 'That's putting it mildly, sweetie,' she drawled, running a red-tipped hand through her vivid cloud of hair. 'Sorry, but when your health starts getting in the way of your work, I have to step in.'

Laura's eyes flickered away from her. She didn't

want to answer any questions, and she didn't want to offend Carly. Difficult, she thought, resting her head in her hands.

'Your nerves are in a mess,' Carly drawled, 'your face looks like old grey washing and you've got rings under your eyes the size of Ferris wheels.'

Laura felt a slight smile touch her mouth. 'Thanks,' she murmured wryly.

Carly's mouth lifted at the corners. 'That's okay, kid. I'm hot on the compliments today.' She sipped her coffee, then looked back at Laura. 'You don't have to tell me what's wrong,' she laughed wryly, 'I can see you aren't going to anyway.'

Laura smiled but did not reply.

Carly tapped an imaginary cigar. 'I'm gonna make you an offer you can't refuse,' she announced in a mock Marlon Brando voice.

Laura laughed. 'What's that?'

Carly slid off the desk. 'Take the rest of the day off, sweetie.'

Laura stared at her in amazement. 'That's very kind of you, Carly. Thank you very much.'

Carly's red mouth lifted. 'These generous impulses do not come straight from my little golden heart,' she drawled. 'The boss is coming over this afternoon, and I don't want him thinking we've got Sad Sam hiding out in the office.'

Laura grinned, standing up and putting her things away.

Carly looked back at her. 'Take my advice—go home and slap a couple of steaks on those eyes. You look like somebody socked you one!'

Laura left the office a moment later, still smiling

slightly from Carly's remark. She passed a shop which had large, very cruel mirrors in the window. Laura eyed herself critically, then pulled a face. I do not look my best, she thought gloomily, walking on.

She took the tube home, emerging from the station feeling tired. The sun was high in the clear blue sky, and it burned down on everything in sight. The tarmac shimmered as cars drove along the road, the sun reflecting off doors, windows and roofs.

Laura stood at the bus stop with two little old ladies who clutched their wicker shopping baskets, eyeing her with passing disapproval. They muttered among themselves, peering around through their fine-rimmed glasses.

Laura smiled hesitantly, and received a smile in return from the old lady wearing the green hat. Laura sighed, looking away. It was strange how a smile from a perfect stranger made one feel instantly better.

Out of the corner of her eye, Laura caught a movement, and saw the silver glitter of the sun as it winked off the roof of a limousine. Her heart began to beat in crazy disturbed movements. She looked around for sanctuary, her eyes moving quickly as she searched for somewhere to hide. There was nowhere. The limousine glided to a halt in front of the bus stop.

The sun reflected off the car door as Jake got out. He stood tall, looking over the roof of the car at her, his eyes glittering.

'Get in,' he commanded.

Laura shook her head, turning her face away from him. Her pulse began to thud, her breath coming faster.

'Get in,' he repeated.

She ignored him, her face averted. She had the two old ladies' attention now. They were looking from her to Jake and back again with undisguised interest.

Jake strode round to where she stood and towered over her. 'Get in the car, Laura,' he said, his face grim and unsmiling.

She swallowed on a dry throat. 'No.'

'If you don't get in the car, I'm going to pick you up and carry you in,' he promised in a calm voice. 'Do I make myself clear?'

She shrugged, keeping her expression blank. 'Do what you please,' she said nonchalantly.

She didn't think he'd do it, of course. Not in front of all those people. She gasped as he swung her into his arms and carried her, legs kicking, over to the car.

'Well!' exclaimed one of the old ladies, nodding knowledgeably at her friend, who peered at Laura, looking shocked.

Jake dumped her unceremoniously in the front seat, and was in the seat beside her before she had a chance to fumble for the door handle.

'Don't try it,' he warned, pulling her hands away from the door handle.

The engine roared into life and they pulled away from the bus stop. Laura rubbed her wrists, glaring at him. 'Who the hell do you think you are? You can't go around abducting me whenever you feel like it!'

Jake smiled thinly. 'Just watch me.'

She looked out of the window, calming herself as much as she could. 'You realise,' she said in a controlled voice, 'that I can get an injunction against you if you don't leave me alone?'

He glanced briefly at her, the powerful mouth straight. 'I'd like to see you try.'

Her lips tightened as she caught the taunting note in his voice. 'You won't have to wait long,' she said, knowing that it was a lie. 'I'll do it as soon as I get back to the office.'

He looked at her as they stopped at a set of traffic lights. 'Really?' His voice was soft, but it carried an underlying thread of menace which warned her that his temper was still as volatile as ever. 'We should be there in half an hour. I'll watch you while you ring your solicitors.'

Her eyes widened as she listened to what he was saying. 'The office?' she echoed, her brow marring in a frown. 'But I've got the afternoon off!'

Jake shook his head. 'Not any more. I'm taking you back there now.'

She leaned forward. 'What do you mean, you're taking me back there? Carly said I could have the afternoon off because I wasn't feeling very well.'

Jake glanced at her briefly, his eyes flickering over her face, taking in the pallor of her cheeks, the hollows beneath her eyes. 'You look terrible,' he said bluntly, his tone crisp as he turned back to look at the road ahead of him.

Laura compressed her lips. 'Thanks,' she said acidly. 'You're so good for my ego.'

He gave a harsh crack of laughter, but the laughter did not reach those cold blue eyes. 'Ego?' he queried. 'You have no ego.'

Laura controlled her temper, sitting rigidly in her seat, her hands clenched at her sides. 'Don't bet on it,

Jake,' she said tightly. 'I have a lot more confidence than you give me credit for.'

His gaze flicked to her for a few brief seconds. 'You're so eaten up with self-pity, you can't believe in yourself any more,' was all he said in that deep, smoky voice.

'That's a lie!' she snapped. 'I'm not that weak, Jake, I'm not going to let you carry on pushing me around like this.'

A smile touched his lips. 'And how do you intend to stop me?' he asked softly.

She looked away from him. 'I'll find a way.'

Jake shook his head slowly, his lean tanned hands sliding over the wheel as they turned a corner. 'You might as well admit it, Laura,' he said grimly, 'I'm stronger than you. You can't beat me.'

She looked at him then, her eyes tracing the hard bones of his face, the cool, steady eyes, the powerful jaw and level mouth. 'You may be physically stronger than me,' she said quietly, 'but you can't force me into trusting you or believing you.'

His upper lip moved in a cold sneer. 'No, because you don't trust anyone, do you, Laura?'

Her gaze moved away from him again, turning to look out of the window at the sunlit streets which flashed past with such painful clarity. 'Can you blame me?' Her voice was quiet, almost a whisper.

He studied her as he changed gears, the strong brown hand close to her, the gold watch he wore peeping out from beneath the crisp white cuff, little black hairs straying over on to the beginning of his wrist. 'You were only let down once. But you can't face the fact that it isn't going to happen every time.' He spoke as quietly as she had done. 'You think men will always let you down.' The car put on a spurt of speed. 'But you're wrong.'

Her hands plucked restlessly with the folds of her skirt. 'You're such an expert,' she said sarcastically.

There was a sudden flash of anger in the hard blue eyes, but it was gone as quickly as it had appeared. 'If you had any backbone, you would have forgotten your father by now,' he told her coldly.

She looked up, her face whitening at his words. 'So easy for you to say, isn't it, Jake?' she said tightly. 'You can't begin to imagine what it was like.'

His face tightened, the blindingly blue eyes filled with sparks of anger. 'Stop it!' he bit out.

Laura glared at him. 'Stop what?'

'Wallowing in self-pity.' He spoke with veiled contempt in the dark tones of his voice.

She stared at him in disbelief, his words echoing in her ears. Was he right? Was she spending her life thinking only of the past? Then she remembered their wedding day. No, he was just trying to find a way round her by making her feel in the wrong.

They were stuck in a traffic jam at St Paul's, and Jake turned to look at her, his black head tilted to one side. 'You don't trust anyone around you, but sooner or later you're going to have to do just that. You can't go through life suspecting everyone's motives.'

Her head came up at that, her eyes bright with anger. 'Meaning you, I suppose?' she snapped.

'Me and anyone else who happens to be male,' came the terse reply.

'Oh, I see,' she said, her voice trembling, 'I've got it in for the entire male sex now, according to you.'

'How else do you explain your inbuilt distrust of men?' he asked tightly.

Her temper flared. 'I don't,' she said angrily, 'because I don't have to explain anything to you.'

'Don't you?' The car jerked to a halt a few doors away from her office, and Jake switched the engine off, turning to look at her with a face which could have been carved from granite.

Laura suddenly felt very small and helpless as she looked at that dark, forbidding face. She shivered. 'No,' she said huskily, 'I don't.'

He stared down at her broodingly. 'One day,' he said, his voice soft but with a thread of violence running through it, 'I'll make you listen to me. You won't escape me for ever.'

She stared at him for a moment in silence, then turned and fumbled for the door handle, her body tense. The humidity of the sunny afternoon struck her as soon as she stepped into it. She waited while Jake got out of the car and came round to her side.

He took her arm in a possessive grip and began to lead her over to the entrance of the office.

'Jake,' she said as they walked into the lifts on the ground floor, 'you didn't tell me. Why are we here?'

He turned cold eyes on her as the lift took them to the fourth floor. 'You'll find out soon enough.'

'Is it something to do with Rupert?' she asked hopefully.

Jake ignored her, stepping out of the lift at the fourth floor and leading her down the corridor towards Rupert's office. Laura followed him with apprehension. What did he have planned for her? He wouldn't have gone to all this trouble to get her here if he didn't have something in mind. Something very important.

He ushered her into Rupert's office and went over to shake Rupert's hand. Laura watched, closing the door behind her. Jake went to stand by the window, looking coolly authoritative in the dark pin-striped suit and crisp white shirt.

Rupert beamed at her. 'Laura my dear,' he said, not sensing the undercurrents which ran between them, 'I'm glad Mr Ashton reached you in time. You remember him, don't you?'

'Oh, I remember him,' she said between her teeth, her eyes bright with anger.

Rupert gestured to a chair opposite him. 'Sit down, my dear, sit down.'

She crossed the room and sat down, her mind spinning dizzily as she tried to work out what Jake had planned for her.

Rupert beamed again. 'I have some exciting news for you—perhaps the biggest step forward in your career here at *Style*.'

Laura swallowed. What was going on? She looked at Jake, but his face was unreadable.

'Mr Ashton,' continued Rupert, his hollow face wreathed in smiles, 'has offered us the chance of a really first-class interview. It will be held in a week's time, and the people to be interviewed are Theresa Phillips and her new husband, Russ Taylor.' He peered at Laura to see what effect this news would have on her.

She tried hard to look excited. She smiled stiffly, her hands clenching into fists, but her face was white and her eyes were angry. She wanted to scream in helpless frustration, but she could only sit still and listen to Rupert.

'If we're quick,' Rupert was saying, 'we might even get it into August's issue. The sooner we have it in print the better, don't you agree, Laura?'

'Absolutely,' she agreed tightly. Out of the corner of her eye she could see Jake's slow smile of triumph. She controlled a desire to hit him.

'What's more,' Rupert was beaming profusely, 'you are the lady who'll be doing the interview. Mr Ashton specifically asked for you. He has great confidence in you.'

I'll bet he does, Laura thought angrily. 'How kind of him,' she snapped before she could stop herself.

The sarcasm was lost on Rupert. 'Oh yes,' he agreed blithely, 'and I wouldn't want you to let him down. This interview is very important. You'll be staying at Theresa Phillips' house in France in order to get it done properly. She wants you there for a week, because this interview has to be top-rate.'

Laura's heart almost stopped at his words. Her eyes widened, her stomach churning in sudden fear. 'A week?' she asked breathlessly, 'at her house?'

Jake smiled, his hard mouth twisting. 'She's only just bought the house. I get the feeling she wants to show it off.'

'A week?' she repeated incredulously. Now she understood why Jake had gone to such lengths to get her on this interview. She wasn't an experienced reporter. It must have been hard persuading Rupert to let her take it on.

Rupert leant forward, smiling. 'Don't you worry, Mr Ashton will be there to supervise matters.'

Laura regarded him with intense irritation. That was what she was afraid of.

'There'll also be a photographer. We'll send him down with you as soon as we have confirmation on who's free and who isn't.'

Jake was watching her with those piercingly blue eyes. He was watching her being backed into a tight corner, and he was enjoying every minute! She looked across at him, her eyes filled with unspoken hatred.

She had to get out of there. Her temper was rising. She felt so angry, so humiliated, that she thought her head might blow off. She stood up abruptly, struggling for self-control.

'I'll look forward to hearing the rest of the details as soon as they're worked out.' She almost choked on the words, her lips tight as she smiled stiffly.

Rupert beamed. 'Good, good,' he said, moving away from the desk. 'In the meantime, Mr Ashton would like a quick word with you. He wants to tell you all the angles he wants on the interview.'

Laura turned her head slowly to meet Jake's gaze. 'I see,' she said between her teeth.

'Well,' Rupert moved to the door, 'I'll leave you to discuss things.'

He left the room, and Laura and Jake faced each other in bitter, hostile silence.

She took a deep breath, and, without looking at him, said, 'What's this in aid of, Jake? The Victory March? Come to crow over your triumph, have you?'

'Why should I crow over something which you should look upon as your triumph?' he asked her coolly. 'As Rupert said, it could be the biggest step of your career.'

Laura shook her head slowly, her eyes fixed on the side of the desk, blocking Jake's tall, lean body from her view. 'Don't try to patronise me, Jake—I'm not interested. Save your smooth talk for some other occasion.'

He took two lazy steps forward, sliding one hand into his pocket as he regarded her with cold blue eyes. 'You would have taken the job quite happily if I hadn't been involved,' he pointed out.

Her head came up at that. 'Damned right I would!' she flung. 'But then you are involved, and that puts a very different angle on the job. I don't want anything to do with you.'

Jake shrugged broad shoulders. 'So you keep telling me.' The cool voice held a note of disdain which immediately put Laura's back up.

'Then why don't you pay any attention to what I say?'

He smiled, the hard mouth moving upwards in a cold sneer. 'I thought you were a dedicated journalist. Obviously you're not as professional as you would have everyone believe, or you wouldn't let my presence interfere with your work.'

Her lips tightened. 'I don't need your help, thank you very much!' she snapped angrily, 'I've been managing without your help for quite some time. I'm sure I can manage without it now.'

He took a further step towards her, one jet-black brow raised derisively. 'You think so?' he queried.

'Quite adequately,' she snapped back.

'Been doing a lot of personal interviews lately, have you?' he asked with a cold twist of the mouth.

Her eyes flared a bright angry green, 'I'll get there eventually, Jake,' she told him tightly, 'but I'd prefer to get there on my own merits, not under your beneficent radiance.'

If she didn't get out of that room fast, she would do something she would regret. Her temper was rising fast, and in the face of Jake's cold mockery, she knew she wouldn't be able to control herself for much longer.

'It could take a long time that way,' Jake pointed out. 'Don't forget—it helps to have friends in high places.'

She eyed him with distaste. 'I wouldn't class you as a friend.'

'As you please,' he drawled mockingly. 'It helps to have lovers in high places.'

Hot colour flooded into her face and she stared at him, her eyes hating him. 'You bastard!' she breathed, her voice trembling with the force of her anger. 'You aren't my lover.'

The sensual mouth moved in a cruel smile. 'Not yet.'

'Not ever!' she flung angrily.

'I'll get you in the end, Laura,' he promised softly. The hard, masculine face was filled with cold determination, and a chill of fear went running through Laura's spine. He meant it.

'I'd rather die!' she flung desperately, trying to refute his words with her anger.

He smiled unpleasantly, his blue eyes cold. 'You wouldn't be much use to me dead,' he pointed out with a flick of his lashes which sent his gaze skimming down over her soft, trembling body.

Her hands clenched and unclenched at her sides. She turned on her heel, her eyes blazing with frustrated temper, and walked swiftly to the door, her head held high, her back stiff. She refused to stay in that room with him for another moment. The insults he was throwing at her were unbearable!

Jake moved swiftly round the desk, his long strides covering the distance between them in seconds. His hand clamped her arm in a biting grip just as she reached for the door handle.

'Going somewhere?' he drawled mockingly in her ear.

'I have to get back to the office,' she clipped out, her words jerky as her throat choked with anger.

He stood behind her, his powerful body almost touching hers, and she felt his overwhelming strength threatening her. His breath fanned her hair. 'I want a word with you.' The deep smoky voice sent a frisson of alarm shooting through her.

'You always do,' she replied, forcing her courage to stay with her. 'But right now, I don't particularly welcome your company.'

'You have a poor memory, my dear,' he drawled unpleasantly. 'I always get what I want—or had you forgotten?'

Her head bent, Laura replied bitterly, 'I haven't forgotten.'

Jake whirled her to face him, his fingers biting into her arm.

'You'll never let me forget, will you, Jake?' she said, her voice scathing as she studied him.

'No,' he said softly, 'I'll never let you forget.'

There was a short, very intense silence. The hard, masculine face was close to hers. She stared at him, feeling an almost uncontrollable urge to reach out and run her fingertips over the close-shaven jawline. She averted her eyes, knowing her feelings had shown through.

Jake caught her chin with one long sinewy hand and thrust her head back, tilting her face towards him. The shrewd blue eyes focussed on her, and a smile moved the sensual mouth.

'Something wrong, Laura?' he murmured.

She stared, mesmerised for a moment. He knew. He knew that being with him was feeding her tormented passion for him.

Her eyelids fluttered down, her lashes brushing her cheeks. 'No, nothing,' she muttered shakily, her face running with hot colour.

The atmosphere between them was steadily changing. Laura bent her head, fighting the emotions building inside her.

'May I go now?' she asked weakly.

'Why the rush, Laura?' Jake asked softly, his hand moving her face back to look at him. 'What are you frightened of?'

She swallowed. He was so close to her. 'I'm not frightened of anything,' she denied, her voice trembling.

He smiled, the hard mouth cruelly insolent. 'Then why are you trembling?'

Laura twisted her head away. 'Please, Jake. . . .' her voice throbbed with sick panic.

The lean fingers bit into her jaw as he pushed her head back. He considered her from heavy lids. 'I think,' he said, one long finger stroking her lips, parting them gently, 'that you're frightened of yourself.'

She shook her head dumbly.

'I think you are,' he murmured, studying her with

shrewd blue eyes. 'I also think,' he added, his mouth brushing tantalisingly against hers, 'you want me to kiss you.'

Her heart stopped beating for a split second, then kicked back into life with crazy, disturbed movements.

His lips brushed teasingly backwards and forwards, their movements sensual and exciting. His tongue snaked out swiftly, touching her lips. 'Like this,' he murmured against her mouth.

She began to respond. Her heart was racing, her body aching for his touch, his kiss.

'And this,' he murmured, his hands sliding sensuously down her back to caress her hips, pressing her closer to him.

Her breath was coming faster, her lips moving in swift rhythm to his, her eyes half closed. Jake groaned from deep within his throat, his arms moving round her, pressing her against his hard, lean body.

'Oh, Laura . . .' he muttered thickly, 'you drive me insane!'

The kiss deepened to a slow, burning heat which spread through her body, filling her with a honeyed excitement. Laura whimpered, her soft, feminine body submissive in Jake's arms, and her hands went to the back of his neck, tangling her fingers in his hair.

Like a butterfly, through her mind, fluttered images which both hurt and disturbed her. She stiffened, her body no longer soft and pliant, her eyes no longer closed.

Jake looked up, his eyes narrowing. Laura felt the heat leave her body, and it was replaced with a strong, bitter hatred. Every time Jake kissed her, laid a hand on her, she would recall that horrifying moment on their wedding day, and the intense physical attraction would be wiped out.

'What is it?' he asked in a deep, smoky voice.

'Stop it,' she whispered between clenched teeth.

He took in the rigidity of her tense body, the distaste in her flashing green eyes, and the harsh planes of his face grew harder, his hands tightening momentarily on her body.

She thought he was about to say something, but at that moment they both heard the outer door open, and Rupert talking to his secretary in a bluff, cheerful voice. Laura broke away from Jake as the door opened and Rupert came in.

Rupert looked from one to the other, his thin, hollow face jolly and cheerful. 'Everything settled?' he enquired, not sensing the undercurrents of tension which ran between them.

Jake nodded curtly, shoving his hands into his pockets and staring down at Laura's stricken face.

She seized her chance of escape. 'Yes, thank you, Rupert,' she managed to say, her throat dry and tight. 'Excuse me, I have to get back to Features.'

She fled out into the cool corridor. Never again, she vowed, would she allow herself to be in the same room as Jake. Every action he made was calculated beforehand, his cruel, shrewd brain cunning. He knew she was still attracted to him, and he was playing on that weakness. What he didn't know was that her mind was acting as a block to her body. Whenever Jake touched her, a series of painful memories coursed before her eyes, and she had to break away from him.

Well, she wouldn't give him the chance to kiss her

again. Not if she could stop him. A frown marred her brow, and she faltered. Could she stop him?

CHAPTER FIVE

PARIS was enchanting. It was filled with life, and love; charm and beauty—it was a miraculous, enticing very feminine city which beckoned with one hand, pushing away with the other, retaining its hold on you with a sly, secretive smile.

Laura looked out of the window with an enraptured expression, breathing in the scent of the beautiful avenues and boulevards, lined with fresh green trees which melted against the clear blue July sky. The large Citroën taxi swung out of the boulevard into the shining haze of the Place de la Concorde, glittering in the hot sunlight.

Cars vied with each other, horns blasting impatiently as they drove around the large obelisk in the centre of the square, the sun glinting off their roofs and windows as drivers leaned out of the windows, angry streams of French issuing forth with typical Gallic enthusiasm.

Laura smiled as she glanced across at the Tuileries Palace. How different from the scenes here a few centuries ago! She could almost envisage the beautiful Marie-Antoinette going nobly to the guillotine in this very square, while crowds of unruly peasants sat watching, their lined faces filled with smug cruelty as they sent the elegant young Queen to her death.

She grimaced. She felt as though she herself were

off to the guillotine. Jake had told her he would meet her at the hotel, and she was already an hour late. But it wasn't her fault; it had been the fault of the ground staff at Heathrow Airport. They were always up to something, and one could only pray that they wouldn't be in a nasty mood when it was your turn to fly from Heathrow. She shrugged. It had only been bad luck that there was a minor dispute that particular day.

She was staying the night in a Paris hotel, owing to the fact that the photographer, Mike, had been unaccountably delayed by another layout. It was too late to cancel the flight by the time they found out, so Jake had booked Laura and himself into a hotel in the centre of Paris.

She sighed and turned to look back out of the window. Sleek, well-groomed Parisiennes tripped gaily along the tree-lined streets, eyed by their male counterparts who sat watching from the vantage point of open-air cafés. They moved with the same energetic pace of Londoners, but their beautiful city somehow lent them an air of elegance which was hard to capture in words.

The taxi driver, a rather weatherbeaten-looking man, caught her eye in the rear-view mirror and smiled, his eyes twinkling with infectious charm.

'You like Paris, *non*?' he asked, smiling.

Laura returned the smile. 'It's beautiful,' she said simply. What more could one say about a city like this, so full of life and charm?

'*Ah, oui*,' he replied with an exaggerated Gallic shrug. 'Everybody, they fall in love with Paris. She is irresistible.'

They turned into the Place Vendôme, and Laura looked up at the tall, imposing column in the centre of the road. Cobbled streets lay all around, lending that timeless elegance to the surroundings.

Napoleon Bonaparte looked down from the top of the column, his head set with a look of haughty disdain as he regarded the strange movements of the lesser mortals below him. Laura smiled, and turned her head as the driver pulled up outside a large hotel.

A liveried doorman came down the marble steps, his red and grey uniform spotless and neatly pressed, and opened the door for her, saluting as he did so. 'Bienvenue, mademoiselle!' he said, already moving to take the case from the driver.

Laura paid the taxi, and walked into the cool marble foyer with a sigh of relief. She loved the summer, but sometimes it could get a little too hot, and that made her uncomfortable. Gold and marble surrounded her, and she breathed in the luxurious cool of the hotel.

She walked to the reception desk, her eyes darting apprehensively in search of Jake's well-shaped black head. He was nowhere to be seen. Her step faltered, and she swallowed. What if he wasn't here to meet her? She would hate to spend a day totally alone in a strange city.

The man at the desk smiled. 'Ah, Mademoiselle Hadleigh,' he said with a flourish, producing a form which he handed to her to fill in. He watched while she signed the form, and then said, 'Monsieur Ashton is waiting in the residents' lounge.'

Her hand faltered, and she looked up, her face whitening a little. Then she handed him the form, pulling herself together enough to give him a brief smile. She turned and walked towards the lounge, clutching her key in tight fingers.

So he was waiting for her. She swallowed. She desperately hoped there would be no more arguments—she had had enough.

Jake stood out from the other people immediately. There was a dynamic energy which surrounded him, an aura of ruthless power and authority which made him stand out from the crowd instantly.

The hard-boned face was enigmatic as he stood up. Laura walked towards him, her face deliberately controlled, her eyes blank.

'Laura.' The blue eyes glittered over her as he inclined his well-shaped black head. 'Did you have a good flight?'

She forced a smile. 'It was okay once we got off the ground. I had to wait an hour while they dithered about—too many planes taking off or something.'

'Air traffic control, or ground staff?' he asked, gesturing towards a seat opposite him. Laura sat down, watching as Jake sat down too, stretching his long legs in front of him, the hard lithe body relaxed as he surveyed her with hard eyes.

She shrugged. 'I don't know. Air traffic control, I expect. We had to queue up behind some jumbo jets on the runway for ten or fifteen minutes.' She wanted to keep the casual conversation up. She had no wish whatsoever to touch on personal subjects.

'They do tend to get pretty crowded at this time of year,' Jake agreed, his black lashes flickering as they travelled lightly over her body, taking in the slender form in the light cotton summer dress.

Their eyes met, and Laura caught her breath. He was devastating. Jake studied her for a second, then crooked one long finger, and a waiter appeared at their side. 'Martini?' Jake queried, one black brow arched.

She nodded. 'Please.'

The waiter disappeared again like a genie, and Jake looked back at her. 'I spoke to Theresa this morning,' his voice was crisp, precise, 'I explained the situation to her, and she seemed rather disappointed. I think she was looking forward to it. She likes a lot of attention, which is why she was so quick to agree to the interview and photo session.'

Laura shrugged. 'It's only a slight delay. Mike couldn't get away for another day. It's an important layout that he wants to finish, and it just can't be helped.'

Mike Jenson had been chosen for the work because of the excellent reputation he had built up in the last two years. He was a carefree, very casual young man of twenty-four, and had been doing a lot of freelance work for *Style* over the last year.

Jake was watching her closely with incisive blue eyes. 'You know him well?' he asked.

She shrugged again. 'Reasonably so. We've worked together on one or two occasions, and he pops into the office a lot.' She liked Mike; he was great fun to be with. He had a never-ending supply of both energy and absurd jokes, and was well endowed with a sense of the utterly ridiculous, which certainly made a working day seem shorter.

Jake watched her for a moment through heavy lids, then picked up the crystal tumbler in front of him, sipping his whisky, his head tilted back to expose the tanned column of his throat.

'I told Theresa we'd be down at around three tomorrow,' Jake told her. He replaced the glass on the table with a sinewy hand. 'As soon as the photographer arrives, we'll leave. You'd better be ready and packed by the time he gets here.'

'Mike told me he'd get down here at around eleven,' she told him. 'But with the planes in the summer rush, he might be late.'

Jake shrugged, the movement drawing her eye to the powerful muscles beneath the smart summer blazer he wore. Dark blue, it was teamed with beautifully cut grey trousers and an open-necked sexy blue and white striped shirt.

'Whatever time he gets here should be okay,' Jake said slowly. 'I just want to have enough time to eat before leaving.' He smiled slowly. 'I don't like rushing meals.'

Laura gave him a polite little smile. She was always so nervy when he was around, his very presence making her prickle apprehensively.

He looked up, his black brows drawn in a frown. 'Are you busy this afternoon?'

She eyed him warily. 'Well, no, not really.'

'Good. I thought I'd take you around Paris, as we're both free this afternoon. We could visit a couple of English bookshops I know.' He gave her a lazy smile, his eyes twinkling. 'You always were the worst book-worm I'd ever met.'

She smiled against her will. 'Is that so?' Her heart skipped a little beat. He remembered! She told herself to stop being so silly, but her cheeks were flushed with pleasure.

Jake laughed softly. 'There's Shakespeare's down by Notre Dame, which sells English books by the score, and then, of course, there's W. H. Smith's in the Rue de Rivoli.'

'W. H. Smith's? In Paris?' She laughed at his nod.

Jake eyed her through hooded lids. 'I'll take you there this afternoon.'

'Thank you, that's very kind.'

He arched one arrogant brow. 'Not at all. I'm not busy this afternoon, and I was thinking of visiting the place myself. There's no reason why I shouldn't take you with me.'

He crooked one long finger and the waiter scurried over. 'The bill,' Jake said crisply, and the waiter hurried off to return with the bill which Jake signed in bold black strokes. He stood up lazily, putting a note on the table as a tip.

'Ready?' He watched Laura as she hastily finished her drink.

Laura replaced the glass and stood up.

Jake took her arm with one sinewy hand. 'I suggest you go up to your room and unpack. I'll collect you in half an hour, then I'll show you how to get to Smith's.' His gaze flickered in her direction as they left the lounge. 'Unless you'd prefer to go to Shakespeare's?'

'Either.' She smiled. 'Both. I'm curious to see inside, see what they're like.'

He walked with her to the lift and pressed the call button. The doors slid open with a muted swish. 'Well, we can go to Shakespeare's later. It's open till late, and Notre Dame looks far more beautiful at night—all of Paris does.'

Laura hesitated. Now that definitely was not a good idea. Being with Jake all evening would only end in more arguments. Besides, she told herself, going out in the evening would defeat the object of the exercise. If she was out, she would have no need of books.

She stepped into the lift with a brief smile. 'We'll see how it goes,' she conceded.

Jake inclined his head, turning to walk away from the lift as the doors closed again. Laura pressed the sixth button and waited as the red numbers marked her ascent.

She was delighted by the room she had been given. Decorated in polished wood with gold and white upholstery and huge canopied bed in blue and white, it seemed as though she had stumbled into Wonderland. She clasped her hands together in delight, looking out of the huge French windows on to the busy hum of Parisian life below her. There was little point in unpacking if she would only be here for a night. She took two outfits from her suitcase and hung them in the wardrobe, hoping the creases would drop out.

She took a quick shower, stripping her clothes off and stepping into the smoked glass cubicle. The warm jets of water cascaded over her, and she raised her head to meet the needles of water, smiling as the torrents of water fell over her face and hair.

Jake knocked on the door just as she finished dressing. 'Just a minute!' she called out, eyeing her reflection in the mirror.

She looked cool in a white off-the-shoulder lace blouse tucked into tight white jeans, her golden tan accentuated by the clear, crisp colour. She felt good, and smiled. It was something about Paris that made her feel instantly more alive.

'Hello,' she said brightly as she opened the door to Jake, turning back to pick up her handbag.

He stood in the doorway, looking tall and sexy in black jeans and white silk shirt, open at the neck.

'Enchanting,' he said smokily, his blue eyes glittering as they swept over her.

Laura met his gaze with a little smile, her full pink mouth curving. 'Thank you,' she said.

He laughed softly, raising one jet black brow with amusement. 'You're in a good mood,' he observed as she moved towards the door.

She stopped as she reached him, not daring to move too close in case she brushed against the hard length of his body. 'Yes,' she returned, 'I think it's Paris. It makes me feel more alive.'

A smile touched the hard mouth, and he inclined his black head. 'Very true,' he murmured, a flick of the black lashes sending his gaze skimming down over her.

There was a little silence filled with a strange tension. Laura took a deep breath and moved past him into the corridor outside.

Jake pushed away from the door frame with lazy grace. 'Got everything?' he asked as they walked to the lift.

She nodded but said nothing. They went down to the ground floor and walked through the foyer, which was veiled in a discreet hush. A doorman sprang to attention as they stepped into the street.

'*Taxi, monsieur?*' he enquired.

Jake glanced at Laura. 'Shall we take a taxi or walk?'

She shielded her eyes from the rays of the sun with one hand. 'How far is it?'

He shrugged. 'Not that far, but it's quite a walk if you're tired,' he told her briskly.

She thought for a moment, then she gave a little smile. 'Can we take a taxi?'

He smiled, the sensual mouth curving slightly. 'Of

course.' He turned to the doorman, who quickly hailed a taxi for them.

They spoke little during the ride. Laura looked out of the window, noting with amusement that French drivers were far worse than English ones. They seemed to play their own little version of bumper cars with each other, charging around all over the road with no consideration for their fellow drivers. She smiled as she caught the tail end of a few nasty-sounding words which were being directed at their own taxi.

Jake stepped out of the taxi outside the shop, and took her hand, helping her out too. He paid the driver and looked round at Laura, noting her pleased expression as she looked up at the shop. 'Like being in England again, isn't it?' he commented as he took her arm.

They wandered around for half an hour, taking their time as they leafed through different books, going from one shelf to another with absorption. Then Jake came over to her side with two or three books under his arm. 'Ready?'

She smiled, following him over to the cash desk. Jake took the books from her.

'No, it's all right,' she protested, laughing as she tried to take the books back. 'I'll pay for my own books.'

Jake silenced her with a speaking glance from those cold blue eyes. 'I'll take care of it,' he told her crisply as he handed over a few notes to the cashier, who watched with a sly smile.

He took her arm again, leading her to another staircase. 'Coffee?'

'Mm,' she nodded. 'Why not?'

They went into a café, taking their places in the mock-Tudor room, and waited while the waitress meandered over to them, pad in hand, a deadpan expression on her face.

Jake ordered their coffees in a crisp, almost perfect accent, his words fluent, his pronunciation excellent. Then he turned back to Laura, leaning back in his seat and resting his hands on the table, palms down. 'So— you've never been to Paris before, I take it?'

She shook her head. 'I went to Calais once on a school trip, but I suppose that doesn't count. That's as far into France as I ever got, I'm afraid. I enjoyed myself, though.' She grinned. 'The teacher in charge went green on the hovercraft and had to rush off to the bathroom!'

Jake allowed a smile to curve his mouth, watching as the waitress placed their coffees in front of them. 'You ran wild, I suppose?'

She nodded, stirring sugar into her coffee. 'Poor man, he couldn't control us after that—he felt too ill.' She shrugged. 'But I've never been to Paris before.'

They sipped their coffee, and Laura wondered why she was sitting here talking so freely to Jake, when she had been so determined to avoid him at all costs.

He watched her through heavy lids. 'So you have no friends here?' he asked casually.

'No,' she smiled. 'Not a soul.'

Jake surveyed her, his black head tilted to one side. 'What did you plan to do tonight?'

She indicated the paper bags beside her filled with books. 'Nothing,' she told him truthfully, 'except have a hot bath and a light read before bed. I can't watch television—I don't speak French.'

The black brows rose in surprise. 'No? I thought you did.'

She shook her head. 'Only schoolroom phrases. I hardly remember any of it.'

'It would be a pity to miss seeing Paris by night,' he murmured, watching her with thoughtful blue eyes, his face enigmatic, his voice crisp. 'Why don't we have dinner together?'

Laura looked up. Last time they had had dinner together had been a disaster. She drew a soft breath. 'I don't think that's a very good idea.'

There was a little silence. She eyed him warily, wishing she could open up his head and see inside it, find out what was going through his mind.

'Paris is even more enchanting by night,' Jake said softly.

She gave him a polite little smile. 'I'm sure it is,' she agreed, avoiding his eyes. 'But I still don't think it would be a very good idea if we saw it together.'

There was another silence, then he said crisply, 'We're stuck together in this city for the night, so we might as well make the most of it. It would be absurd if you stayed in the hotel brooding on the past.'

Her lips tightened. 'I am not brooding on the past!'

Jake spread his hands in front of him. 'Then come out tonight. I've got nothing to do and neither have you.'

She leaned forward, resting her arms on the table. 'Don't try to use me as something to fill in your spare time with, Jake. What do you think I am? A tube of Polyfilla?'

His eyes glittered, darkening suddenly. 'A tube of

Polyfilla is the last thing I would have compared you with,' he said thickly.

Laura opened her mouth to say something, thought better of it, and closed it.

His eyes narrowed as he watched her. 'Are you frightened of me, Laura?' he murmured.

'No, I'm not,' she lied, shivering.

He shrugged. 'Then come out with me tonight.'

She sighed, leaning forward again. 'Look, you must have friends in Paris. Go and visit them. We always end up arguing. I'd rather have a lonely bath than go out with you and argue all night.'

'We'll call a truce,' he told her, leaning back in his chair and studying her calmly.

Laura muttered under her breath, 'Jake, there's no point. . . .'

'Stop arguing,' he broke in crisply. 'We'll have dinner at eight, then walk around Paris for a while.'

It was pointless arguing with him. She eyed him with intense irritation. Maddening man, she thought, sighing. He wouldn't budge an inch once he'd decided on something. And that, thought Laura, is evidently that.

She sat back in her chair, defeated. 'Oh, very well, if you must be so obstinate about it.'

He laughed, standing up and putting some coins on the table with the bill. 'Not obstinate, my sweet,' he said as he led her to the door. 'It's just common sense.'

She eyed him wryly. 'Is that what you call it? I could think of another word, myself.'

Pigheaded, she thought as they left the café, is what I would call it. They walked out into the hot sunshine, and she shaded her eyes, looking up at the sky. 'I'll get sunstroke,' she murmured, half to herself.

Jake studied her. 'You don't like the sun?'

'Not when it's this hot,' she said, screwing up her eyes with discomfort as the sun blazed into them.

'It gets hotter than this in New York. We were going to live there, remember?' He slid a casual glance at her.

Her lips tightened as a stab of pain sliced through her. How could she forget? He had flown her out there for a weekend to see their new house. The memory came back to her crystal clear and she recalled the happiness she had felt on seeing their new home.

'I remember,' she said tightly.

A cold smile twisted his mouth. 'I thought you said you'd forgotten all about me?'

Laura faltered, her step jerky as he spoke. Then she pulled herself together, walking slightly faster. 'Did I say that?' she said in a tight, bored voice, and laughed. 'You see? I'd forgotten I even said it.'

'Of course,' he drawled, thrusting his hands into the pockets of his jeans. 'I'm so forgettable. That's why you're so bitter towards me, isn't it? Because you forget things so easily.'

Laura tightened her lips further. She got the feeling that Jake was deliberately trying to start an argument. Well, she wasn't rising to the bait. Without looking at him, she asked in a cool voice, 'Do you still have the house?'

He looked down at her, his eyes blindingly blue. 'Yes.'

There was a little silence. Laura stopped to look in a shop window, her glance falling on Jake's tall reflection as he stood beside her. 'Why?' she asked casually.

Jake shrugged. 'I don't know. I always seemed too

busy to get around to doing anything about it, so in the end, I just left it as it was.'

She raised her brows. 'Even the furniture? Is that still there?' She remembered the *Swan of Eden* on his wall at the London hotel. If he had had that shipped over here, why not any of the other pieces?

'I had a lot of it transferred to California and London after you left,' he told her crisply. 'There wasn't much point in keeping them in an empty house.'

Her eyes met his in the shop window. 'Why didn't you keep it all there and live in it from time to time?' she asked quietly.

There was a short silence. 'It's too out of the way,' Jake said tersely, beginning to walk away down the street.

Laura hurried after him and fell into step beside him, and they walked back to the hotel in silence.

She was ready at seven-thirty. Dressed in a slim white sheath dress, she looked cool and elegant. Her long red-gold hair fell in shining waves around her shoulders; a vivid cloud around her beautiful face which only held the barest amount of make-up.

Jake knocked on the door at eight, and Laura went to answer it, taking her handbag with her.

The black brows rose as he studied her, his gaze flickering down over her slender figure. A smile touched her mouth. 'Is that what you're wearing?' he said, although it was more of a statement than a question.

She nodded, glancing down at her dress. 'Is anything wrong with it?' she asked.

He watched her through thick sooty black lashes.

'You look ravishing. But you might end up black and blue.'

She frowned. 'Black and blue?' she repeated, puzzled.

He took her arm, leading her over to the lift. 'It doesn't matter. Let's go down to eat, shall we?'

They went down to the restaurant in silence, and the head waiter came hurrying over to them, his face wreathed in smiles as he lead them over to their table.

Laura noticed the covetous glances thrown in Jake's direction. They were indiscreet if not obvious, and she shrugged inwardly. Women always looked at Jake like that, she thought, her eyes running over the hard, muscular body in the well-fitting dinner suit. Jake Ashton was every woman's idea of the eligible bachelor. His power overawed them, his ruthless streak excited them. Wealthy playboy, jet-setter, ruthless tycoon—his sexuality was stamped on every line of that hard, devastating face, and he made good use of it. Women fell like ninepins when he so much as looked in their direction with those sexy, glittering blue eyes.

He ordered for both of them, keeping the meal light and simple—salade niçoise, then steaks, served to them by attentive waiters who hovered, pouring wine and enquiring if everything was all right. Laura wasn't very hungry.

Jake watched her as she toyed with a piece of steak. 'Not hungry?' he asked.

She smiled, putting her fork down on the plate, her hand curling round the long stem of her wine glass. 'I think it's the travelling. It always puts me off my food.'

But it wasn't that. It was the tension which sprang

up between her and Jake every time they were within a
five-mile radius of each other. There were shock waves
of energy that crackled between them almost tangibly.

Jake signed the bill, and waited while she stood up.
Then he took her hand and led her out into the crisp
summer air.

They took a taxi from outside the hotel, driving
through the streets of Paris which were still crowded,
even though it was nearly nine in the evening. Dusk
was a long way off still, and people ran through the
streets, laughing, enjoying the last hours of daylight.

The taxi stopped at a crossroads, and Laura looked
across the road in amazement. Hordes of jean-clad
people were crowding around a group of musicians
who were playing outside a tall building on the corner.
Jake helped her out of the taxi.

'Where are we?' she asked, looking towards the
happy scene on the other side of the street.

'The Boulevard St Michel.'

'Who are all those people?' she asked as they crossed
the road.

He looked across at her. 'Just a group of holiday-
makers out enjoying themselves.'

She looked up at him with a hesitant smile. 'Can we
go over there and listen for a while?'

'If you wish,' he said, allowing a smile to curve his
mouth.

They walked over to the crowd, and stood listening
to the loud rock music issuing forth. The atmosphere
was lively and happy, and Laura found herself tapping
her feet in time to the music, a smile on her lips,
looking at the faces of the people there.

She peeped at Jake from beneath her lashes, and

their eyes met. 'Enjoying yourself?' he asked in a deep, sexy voice.

She nodded, grinning. 'It's fantastic,' she replied. 'Are they buskers?'

He shrugged. 'Perhaps. They always come to play here—but not necessarily the same group every time.' His glance flickered over the crowd, then stopped, and Laura watched his eyes narrow. She looked in the direction of his glance to see a young, friendly-looking boy in denim watching her. He grinned at her, and Laura grinned back, amused by his infectious smile.

Jake took her arm and began to lead her away.

'Why are we leaving?' she asked with a frown as they walked away down the street.

He looked down at her with a cold face. 'I thought we'd explore the Latin Quarter,' he said coolly.

Her frown deepened. 'That's not true. You were angry because that boy was smiling at me.' She could have bitten her tongue off once she had said it, but she had been irritated by his possessive handling of her.

His eyes narrowed. 'You don't seem to realise that flirting with strangers in this area will only cause trouble.'

'Don't be so pompous! I wasn't flirting with him. He smiled at me, that was all.'

'And you smiled back,' he reminded her in an unpleasant drawl.

'So what? He was only a boy. What do you expect me to do when someone smiles at me? Poke my tongue out?' She walked beside him feeling intensely irritated by his behaviour. The boy was only being friendly— he could see Jake was with her.

They walked on in silence for a while, then turned

into a long narrow street with tall, decaying buildings, crumbling shutters open on every window, loud music and the sound of voices issuing from every building, echoing in the charming narrow street.

'Where's this?' Laura ventured, looking around her, not daring to glance in Jake's direction in case he was still angry.

'The Latin Quarter,' he said shortly.

Laura pulled a face at his tone, but said nothing. A group of young boys moved towards her, laughing among themselves, eyeing Laura with open admiration. One moved very close to her and pinched her thigh, and she turned to stare after him with irritation.

Jake gave her a speaking glance. Laura ignored it, but by the time they had reached the end of the street, she had been pinched several times.

She looked at Jake. 'Don't you dare say, "I told you so"!'

His eyes widened innocently. 'Me? Why should I say that?'

She eyed him wryly. 'Because I'm black and blue.'

He laughed, his eyes twinkling with amusement. 'Come on, I'll take you to Shakespeare's.'

They strolled along to the Ile de la Cité. By the time they arrived it was growing dark, the lights in Paris shining off the River Seine, making the air of romance seem even stronger. Laura looked out over Paris, feeling suddenly lonely.

Young couples strolled past, happy, their arms linked as they wandered along, talking. Laura eyed them with slight envy. She had no one, and she doubted if she ever would. Jake had let her down so badly that she couldn't see herself ever trusting another

man again. It would be too hard to place her trust in
the hands of any man, knowing the callous way they
could behave.

She eyed Jake sadly. Why had it happened? They
could have been so happy. She had loved him so much
when they first met that she had thought they would
stay together for ever. Her marriage vows had been so
real to her—she had meant every word. But Jake obviously hadn't. She sighed, looking up at him as they
reached the bookshop.

'It's bound to be packed,' he said, looking inside
through the glass windows.

Laura shrugged. 'I don't really need any books,' she
said, trying to shrug off her mood, but her voice came
out dull and flat.

Jake looked at her closely. 'What's wrong?'

She fingered one or two of the books which stood
outside the shop in little rows. 'Nothing,' she said
quietly.

A frown drew those dark brows together over the
top of his strong, arrogant nose. 'Sure?'

She nodded, pulling herself together and giving him
a tight smile. 'Quite sure.' She glanced at the bookshop. 'Let's walk for a while. I'm not really in the
mood for hunting out books.'

The incisive blue eyes studied her for a moment in
silence, then he shrugged. 'As you wish,' he said ex-
pressionlessly. He took her arm again, leading her on
towards the cathedral which rose out of the darkness
like a symbol of hope, the lights of Paris illuminating
it on either side, the air of romance spilling over on to
it.

Laura was silent as they walked. She couldn't

understand why she felt so sad. Perhaps it was just that she was tired, but she didn't really think so. It was being with Jake in this romantic city, seeing other couples who were happy, and knowing that she and Jake could never recapture their own happiness.

It was all too long ago, and one could never walk back to yesterday. She sighed, looking up at the cathedral of Notre Dame. The lights shone on its sculptured lines, leaving it half shadowed, half illuminated by night. It was beautiful, but Laura couldn't respond to its beauty at that moment. She felt too sad.

'Coffee?' Jake indicated a large café opposite them, the red canopy stretching out invitingly.

She shrugged. 'I don't mind,' she said flatly, and Jake looked at her with narrowed eyes.

'Yes or no?' he enquired coolly.

She sighed. 'Why not?' She tried to make her voice sound cheerful, but it wouldn't do as she wanted, and came out flat and dull instead.

Jake gave her a barbed smile. 'Don't bowl me over with enthusiasm,' he said sardonically.

Laura gave him a brief smile. 'Sorry. Yes, let's have some coffee. I could do with a rest.'

He took her arm and led her into the café, seating her opposite him at a large polished wood table. 'Feeling tired?' he asked as he ordered from the waiter.

Laura grimaced. 'A little,' she admitted, looking down at her hands as she rested them on the table.

Jake sipped his whisky, eyeing her with enigmatic eyes. 'I thought we'd stroll along the bridges next,' he suggested. 'The Seine is beautiful at night, and there's a lot to see along the way. A lot of famous landmarks are lit up by night and you can pick them out as you walk along the river.'

Laura couldn't raise much enthusiasm. She looked at him uninterestedly. 'If you like.'

She watched his mouth tighten. 'We don't have to do that. There are plenty of other places we can go if you'd prefer,' he told her in a controlled voice.

Laura sighed again. 'I don't mind. Whatever you like.'

He drew a deep breath and his face tightened further, his mouth a hard firm line. She thought he was about to say something, then thought better of it. She looked down at her coffee and sipped it, grimacing. 'Tastes like mud,' she remarked dully, putting it back in its saucer. She caught Jake's narrow-eyed stare and looked away.

Across the room, someone caught her eye and smiled, and she frowned, feeling a vague sense of familiarity as she studied the person. Then she realised who it was—the young boy who had smiled at her on the corner of the Boulevard St Michel.

The boy gave her a broad, friendly grin, his eyes twinkling, and Laura grinned back, nodding in acknowledgement that she had recognised him.

Jake looked round quickly, following the direction of her gaze. When he turned his head back to look at her, she was amazed by the anger she saw in his eyes. She frowned, taken aback.

Jake finished his whisky, replacing the tumbler on the table with a distinct crash. He thrust some notes on the table and took Laura's wrist in a biting grip.

'What's the matter?' she asked as he dragged her out of the café.

'We're going back to the hotel,' he told her tightly, hailing a taxi and bundling her into the back of it. They rode back to the hotel in a tense, brooding silence.

When they reached her room, he watched while she fumbled in her bag for her key. 'Did you enjoy the evening?' he asked coldly, his hand thrust into his pockets.

Laura nodded, forcing a nervous smile. 'Thank you, yes, I had a lovely time.'

'Liar,' he said bitingly.

She looked up. 'I don't understand,' she faltered.

'I think you do,' he said icily. 'You were all right until we got to Shakespeare's, then you suddenly changed into one of the living dead. Why?'

She shrugged. 'I suppose I was just tired,' she lied.

'I asked you why. Tell me.'

Laura half turned away, avoiding his angry stare. 'I don't know,' she said on a sigh.

His hand gripped her wrist as he spun her back to face him. 'Don't turn your back on me!' he snapped, his mouth biting out the words.

She tugged at her wrist, staring at him with wide, frightened eyes. 'Why are you getting so angry?'

'When I take a woman out for the evening, I don't expect her to be sullen and uncommunicative without telling me what's wrong.'

She eyed him irritably. 'I wasn't sullen,' she protested, still tugging at her captive wrist.

Jake's eyes were narrowed, ice cold and dangerous. 'You were in a nasty temper. You barely said two words to me for an hour, and when you did speak you were either bored or snappy. Now there must be a reason, and I intend to find it.'

She glared at him, her patience running thin. 'What the hell has it got to do with you?'

His smile was cold. 'I told you—when I take a lady out, I expect a little more than sulky remarks and bad temper.'

He had no idea at all of how bad she had felt, he just automatically took the view that she was doing it to spite him. He was an insensitive, unfeeling swine, and she had had enough of him.

'You're forgetting,' she snapped, eyes bright with anger, 'I'm not one of your mistresses. I don't have to smile and put on an act just because you feel condescending enough to take me out.'

His eyes flashed angrily, temper showing in every line of his face. A muscle jerked in his cheek. 'Of course,' he drawled, 'I was forgetting. You're not a lady—you're my wife.'

Her lips tightened. 'Very funny! But it's a rather worn joke, don't you think?'

His eyes were glacial. 'Worn but true. If it had merely been a mood you were in, I could have understood. But you smiled so prettily at that boy, didn't you, my darling? There was no boredom in your eyes when you looked at him.'

Laura gave an exclamation of impatience. 'Don't be so ridiculous, Jake! He was only a boy. I can smile at anyone I want to, and you weren't smiling at me, so I smiled at him.'

His hands tightened on her wrists. 'I'd forgotten what a little flirt my dear wife was. How many other men have you flirted with since we separated? Have there been many? Can you count them all on one hand? Or do all their faces merge into one long line of conquests?'

She struggled to get away from him, recognising the biting anger in his voice. 'I haven't been involved with anyone since you!' she snapped, pulling away from him. 'I couldn't bring myself to look at another man— any man, and that includes you.'

Jake smiled thinly. 'Of course, you're so insecure, aren't you? It's tragic.'

Laura's eyes flashed bitterly. It wasn't her fault she was insecure—if you're standing on a precipice, you get to feeling a little shaky and unsure from time to time—especially if someone keeps trying to push you over the edge of that precipice.

Her lips tightened into a firm angry line. 'I'm not tied to you, Jake, and you know it. If you want to force me into going out with you, there's not much I can do to stop you, you're stronger than me. But I don't have to show any false affection for you, and I don't have to answer to you for anything.'

Jake's eyes blazed. 'How true,' he said thinly. 'But there is one thing you have to do for me, like it or not. You're still married to me legally.'

There was a tense silence. A shiver of alarm ran through her as she stared at him. 'What's that supposed to mean?' Her voice trembled slightly, although she had expected it to sound calm and controlled.

He came closer. 'Oh, I don't think we need go into detail. You know what I'm talking about,' he drawled in an icy voice.

Laura moved her free hand discreetly, keeping her eyes on him all the time as she slid the key into the lock. 'That won't solve anything, Jake,' she said breathlessly.

He gave a mocking laugh that turned her spine to ice. 'I don't give a damn if it solves anything. I find it far more pleasant than walking around Paris.'

She breathed out with relief as she felt the lock click under her hand. She kept her eyes fixed on him.

'I've been patient with you long enough, Laura,' Jake was saying coldly. 'It's time you stopped running.'

She looked down at her arm, which he still held captive, then her eyes flicked back up to his. 'You're hurting me, Jake,' she said quietly, her face submissive.

His grip relaxed slightly, his face taking on a look of triumph as he moved closer to her.

She seized her chance with both hands, pushing him away, knocking him off balance as she opened her door and slipped inside, locking it behind her before he had a chance to move. She leant against the door, breathing harshly.

'Let me in!' Jake's fists hammered noisily on the door.

Laura made a face. He couldn't get at her now. 'Go away!' she replied calmly. 'You'll wake everyone up.'

There was a silence, then his fists hammered once more on the door. 'Open this bloody door before I break it down!' he bit out.

She winced, but turned away from the door, ignoring him as best she could while he continued to knock on the door. Eventually, he gave up. She heard him mutter something unrepeatable under his breath, bang his fist on the door one last time, and turn to walk angrily back down the corridor away from her room.

She sank on the bed, feeling the lonely silence close in on her.

CHAPTER SIX

LAURA tapped her long fingernails on the arm of the gilt chair in which she sat. The residents' lounge was almost deserted at this time of day, and her green eyes were impatient as they slowly wandered over her surroundings. Mike was supposed to have arrived at eleven, and it was now twenty to twelve.

She sighed, resting her book in her lap as she took a sip of coffee. Jake was meeting her down here at twelve, and she didn't like the idea of being alone when he came. She glanced at her wrist watch again, hoping that Mike would arrive soon.

She hadn't seen Jake all day. She had suspected that he would breakfast in the dining room, and she accordingly had eaten in her room. She didn't want to see Jake alone if it was possible to avoid it—she didn't want a discussion or another argument about last night.

'Hello, sexy!' growled a lecherous voice in her ear.

She looked up, startled, then grinned, seeing Mike Jenson's curly brown head bobbing in front of her, his warm brown eyes dancing with merriment.

'You're late,' she accused, standing up, feeling an intense relief in seeing a familiar face. 'What kept you?'

Mike put a casual arm around her, hugging her tight. He sighed exaggeratedly. 'You're not a jealous woman, are you, darling?' he asked with mock penitance.

Laura laughed. 'You're not trying to tell me it was one of your lady friends?' she asked, looking up into his casual, open face.

Mike put a hand to his forehead with a groan. 'They just won't leave me alone,' he told her, grinning, showing all his teeth in perfect detail. 'I can't help it—they're only after my body.'

Laura punched him playfully on the arm. 'Let go, Buster. I want to sit down.'

Mike sat opposite her, stretching his long, gangly legs in front of him and leaning back with a yawn. Laura eyed his T-shirt. It read 'I Am A Sex Symbol.' She grinned.

Mike leaned over and picked up her empty cup, peering into it sadly. 'Oh, look, a lonely cup. It needs a friend.' He beckoned to the waiter, who came hurrying over. 'Two more coffees, please.' He glanced at Laura as the waiter went scurrying off. 'You're paying, you realise.'

She raised an eyebrow. 'Is that so?'

He pulled a face, turning his pockets out. 'Stony broke,' he said sadly. 'Have pity on a starving photographer.'

Laura smiled, her eyes darting past him, then she stiffened. Jake stood watching them from the alcove where the lift was, his face dark and forbidding. She watched him for a moment, their eyes meeting, then she looked away.

'Were you delayed long?' she asked Mike hurriedly, stumbling over the words as she spoke. She wanted to play it casual, make Jake think she wasn't shaken by his appearance. How long had he been standing there?

Mike shook his head, the brown curls flopping over

his brown eyes, giving him the appearance of a playful spaniel. 'Not too long. But it wasn't boring.' He grinned wickedly. 'Julie came to see me off.'

Laura frowned. 'I thought you were seeing Lisa at the moment?'

Mike waved a hand in airy dismissal. 'Oh, her.'

'Poor Lisa!' murmured Laura with a slight smile.

Mike Jenson seemed to have girl-friends coming out of his ears. He only asked two things of them, apparently—that they were ravishing, and that they could none of them string two sentences together. Laura often wondered what his chat-up line was. Maybe he used sign language.

He had often told her, 'Clever women always catch you in the end. Give me a stupid woman every time—it's the only way to stay free.' She smiled now, studying him out of the corner of her eye. He had managed to stay free so far, so maybe he was right.

She felt rather than heard Jake come up behind her. She stiffened, the hair on the back of her neck prickling, and Mike looked up with a surprised expression. He stood up, scratching his head with one long finger.

'Hi,' he said cheerfully. 'I'm Mike Jenson.' He extended a bony hand.

Jake shook his hand, his eyes steely. 'Jenson,' he said tersely, nodding his head in acknowledgement.

Mike raised his brows in silent comment on the icy look in Jake's eyes, then he sat down again, watching as Jake took a seat opposite him.

'Good morning, Laura,' Jake said curtly.

'Good morning,' she replied in a quiet voice, looking down at the polished table in front of her.

'I trust you slept well,' said Jake in a clipped voice,

crooking one long tanned finger. A waiter appeared. 'Whisky,' Jake said curtly.

Laura surveyed him. 'It's not midday yet,' she reminded him in a subdued tone.

His eyes were cold. 'I'm quite well aware of the time.' His voice sniped at her.

Laura shrugged, looking across at Mike, who was watching with great interest. She sighed inwardly. Jake's tone and manner made it only too clear that he was still angry with her. Unless . . . unless he had seen Mike arrive, seen him put his arm around her. But that had only been playful, it was just the sort of thing Mike always did.

She slid a glance at Jake from beneath her lashes. She hoped he hadn't put a different construction on that casual embrace. Mike Jenson was well known as a flirt—a reputation which didn't bother him in the least; he liked to be known as the man who broke many hearts. But Laura would never get involved with someone like him. He was too young for her way of life; too carefree, too thoughtless. He lived only for the present, and appeared to have no serious thoughts at all. Laura thought too much of her future to think seriously of being involved with someone like that. She thought Jake would realise that. She hoped he would know her well enough to see that Mike just wasn't her type. He was strictly for fun, and Laura thought too much to be able to act the way he did.

They decided to have an early lunch at twelve o'clock. Laura looked at Mike with a frown before walking into the restaurant. 'Hadn't you better put a jacket on?' she asked, indicating his T-shirt.

Mike grinned. 'Rubbish. They might think I'm a famous English pop star.'

Laura laughed, her cheeks dimpling. 'Why on earth should they think that?'

They walked towards the dining room, and Mike gave her an impish grin. 'I walk through the Hilton every morning like this, and the doorman thinks I'm an eccentric millionaire pop star.'

Jake raised one black brow. 'I doubt if you'll give the same impression here,' he said crisply, his gaze flickering distastefully over Mike's rather tattered jeans.

Mike pulled a face while Jake's head was turned and they carried on through the dining room. If the waiters disapproved of Mike's clothes, they gave no sign of it. He was a guest of Jake Ashton's and was treated with respect accordingly.

After the meal, Jake went to pick up the keys for the hired car while Laura and Mike stayed in the dining room. Mike recounted some funny stories about a recent photographic layout he had been working on. Laura felt the tension seep out of her once Jake had left the table, and she relaxed a little.

Mike looked at her oddly after he had finished talking, and asked, 'How come you got this job, Laura? You're not exactly the tops at Features—no offence meant.'

'None taken.' She spread her hands in front of her, her mind working quickly. 'I really don't know. Rupert just called me into the office and sprang it on me. I was as surprised as the rest of the staff.'

Mike studied her with those friendly spaniel's eyes, then leaned back in his seat, toying with a spoon. 'I hear tell you know this Ashton guy better than you're letting on,' he murmured, not looking at her.

She remained calm, her face giving nothing away. So there was already talk at the office about her and Jake, was there? She would have to put a stop to that as soon as she got back.

'Who on earth told you that?' she asked, laughing, treating the statement as though it were a joke.

He raised his brows with a smile. 'Oh, a little bird.' He put the spoon on the table, examining it with great interest. 'Said you knew him very well, too. Perhaps you'd even known him for quite some time—without telling your loyal, trustworthy pals at the office about it. Not only that—but you spent quite a while having a tête-à-tête with him on Rupert's birthday at the nightclub.' He grinned at her, his eyes alive with interest. 'Well, what do you say to that, chum?'

Laura took a deep breath. 'Come on, Mike, you know me better than that. I never imagined that you of all people would start believing the gossip in the office.'

He winked at her. 'Got to keep an open mind on these things, Laura. Not that I'm being nosey, of course, just curious.'

She raised one brow. 'Not to mention ridiculous. How could I possibly know Jake Ashton?'

Mike looked unconvinced. 'Hmm. Okay, I won't say another word on the subject.'

They drove to Theresa Phillips' house as soon as Jake returned. Laura sat in the front of the car with him, while Mike scrambled into the back, and they sped off quickly down the autoroute.

Mike chatted for the first part of the journey, telling

Laura jokes about his working life. But gradually his ebullience was worn down by Jake's stony silence. He sat in the back, fiddling with his cameras, checking each of them with those bony hands. He made an occasional remark as the journey lengthened, but his remarks were greeted by polite murmurs from Laura and steely glances from Jake, so he gave up in the end and kept quiet.

Theresa Phillips and Russ Taylor lived in a large house just outside Chateau St Remalard, a small town between Chatres and Alençon. It was just past three o'clock when the car turned up a leafy drive leading up to the house, and Laura gasped with pleasure as the huge white mansion came into view.

Mike let out a long low whistle. 'I wonder if the Queen's in,' he said cheerfully from the back, and was treated to another steely glance from Jake. He pulled a face and Laura stifled a smile, glancing at Jake.

As they stepped out of the car, the front door burst open, and a ravishingly pretty young woman simply radiated out in the bright sunlight. Her long, sun-streaked blonde hair fell into an untamed mane around her shoulders, dazzling the eyes as she moved towards them. Her smile was wide and genuine, and extremely white, suspiciously so in fact. Her heart-shaped face danced with life and laughter, her cat-like green eyes completing her stupendous beauty.

'Jake darling!' she bubbled, going towards him with a bright smile as she spoke, her chatty voice at odds with her glamorous appearance. 'How are you? So good to see you again after all this time. Did you have a good trip? I know the roads can be pretty nasty in July—so many tourists around. Pity about the delay, but at least you got here eventually—no offence meant, and none taken, I hope. We were just ready for your arrival, you see, so it was a bit of a let-down when you rang yesterday to say you wouldn't arrive till today.'

Jake brushed his hard mouth against her velvet-smooth cheek, a smile playing around his lips. 'I see you're on form today, Terry,' he said with amusement.

Theresa flashed her teeth again, patting him playfully on the arm. 'Oh, shut up!' She looked over at Mike. 'Hello, you must be from *Style* magazine. Glad you could make it. I hope you had a good trip down here.'

'Hullo,' said Mike, awestruck.

Theresa cocked her brilliant, sun-haloed head to one side. 'Are you the photographer?' she asked in that chatty Californian accent.

Mike nodded, his eyes popping out on stalks, apparently struck dumb.

Theresa turned to Laura with a bright smile. 'Hi. Come on in, I'll get you all a drink.' She drifted off in a cloud of perfume, hair and chatter. 'I've been sitting around reading magazines waiting for you to arrive, you know. Russ has gone out for the afternoon—he's pottering around the gardens, I think. He does that a lot, I don't know why. Do sit down, make yourselves at home. It's lovely to have visitors, we haven't had many since we moved in and had our housewarming party six months ago.'

Mike couldn't get in the door fast enough. Jake raised an amused eyebrow at Laura and she smiled, following him in to the large drawing room where Theresa stood, still chattering.

Theresa poured them all drinks, pushing her incredible hair back with one tanned hand as she did so. She continued to chatter to them for another twenty minutes without pause. Jake caught Laura's eye on one occasion and smiled. Laura returned his smile, feeling grateful for the ease of tension—the journey in the car had made her feel slightly nervous.

After a while, Theresa glanced at Laura. 'I suppose you'd like to freshen up now,' she said with a wide smile. 'Silly of me not to think about it before, but I was so pleased you'd managed to get here. It's so out of the way, you see—not like living in California.'

Laura smiled. 'Do you prefer it here? It must be much quieter, more peaceful?'

Theresa bubbled with laughter. 'Well, I complain a lot, I know, but I love it here. I wouldn't want to give it up.' She put her drink down on the mantelpiece and crossed to the door. 'Hold on, I'll just grab hold of our housekeeper and plead with her to show you your rooms.'

Laura found herself smiling again. She liked Theresa, she had eased the tension, Laura felt, with her ceaseless chatter. She could see that it would be easy to interview her, so long as she could get her to keep on the same subject for long enough.

'Mrs Winterbottom,' Theresa cooed, her voice reverberating along the hall, 'could you come here a minute?' She turned back to them and said with an impish grin, 'She looks a bit like an army sergeant, but she's terribly sweet. We brought her over from England, and I don't know what we'd do without her.'

Rumblings were heard from the kitchen, followed by the sound of a door opening and heavy footsteps trudging sulkily towards the drawing room. A large, middle-aged woman appeared in the doorway with a face like moulded dough, her wiry grey curls wobbling around on top of her head.

Theresa patted her arm. 'Mrs Winterbottom, this is Miss Hadleigh and Mr Jenson from the magazine, and of course you remember Mr Ashton, don't you?'

Mrs Winterbottom grunted. 'Afternoon,' she said abruptly.

'Would you be terribly sweet and show them to their rooms, for me?' She smiled at the woman. 'There's a dear.'

Mrs Winterbottom eyed Mike with disapproval. 'Yes, madam,' she said, folding her arms and waiting.

Laura and Mike stood up, gathering their things together.

Jake relaxed in the armchair. 'I'll wait till Russ gets back, Theresa,' he told her, resting one long hand on the edge of the chair.

Mrs Winterbottom bustled to the foot of the stairs, followed by Mike and Laura, who exchanged glances.

'Oh,' Theresa's voice stopped them half-way up the stairs, 'dinner will be at seven-thirty. Wear what you like, we don't mind. We'll see you then, unless you want to wander around.'

Laura followed the housekeeper to a large bedroom while Mike walked beside her with an ecstatic look on his face. She walked into her room, looking at it with undisguised delight. Theresa had given her a very pretty room, decorated in shades of pink and lavender.

'She's incredible!' Mike enthused as he leant on the door frame.

'Incredible,' agreed Laura drily.

'Getting this job was a lucky break,' he continued. 'I've always wanted to meet someone like her, it's like winning a trip to Hollywood.'

Mrs Winterbottom's face was rigid with hostile disapproval. 'I'll show you your room now, sir, if you don't mind,' she said in a cross little voice, her eyes fixed on him.

Mike grinned at her. 'Thanks, Mrs W., you're a pal,' he teased, patting her folded arms.

Mrs Winterbottom's lips disappeared with disapproval and her eyes narrowed. 'I'll thank you to call me Mrs Winterbottom,' she said frostily. 'Now, if you don't mind, I have a lot of work to do.'

Mike made a face. 'Lead the way.'

She stomped off down the corridor and Mike waved to Laura. 'See you at dinner.'

Laura shook her head with amusement, and went over to her bed to unpack her bulging suitcase. She hung all the clothes in the wardrobe, setting her cosmetics on the dressing table. When she had finished, she sighed, crossing to look out of the window on to the acres of greenery below her.

The gardens were beautiful in the late afternoon, the sun glittering through the trees, shafts of light picking out rows of rose-bushes which danced in the summer breeze. Laura put her head in her hands, looking out with a smile. She didn't really want to stay in her room all afternoon. She decided to have a quick shower, then go for a walk in the grounds.

She stepped out of the shower, wrapping a large, fluffy bath towel around herself. She found herself thinking of Jake again. Why had he stayed down in the drawing room with Theresa? She shrugged. Perhaps he had just wanted to talk to her for a while—after all, she was signing a new contract with him, and there would be plenty to discuss.

She pinned a loose strand of hair behind her ears, tucking it back into the ponytail her hair was secured in. She went into her bedroom and walked over to the dressing table, sitting down at it with a pensive expression on her face.

Why had Jake gone to such lengths to bring her down here? She still hadn't been able to work out exactly why he had done it. He had known that she wouldn't have been able to give a good excuse to Rupert if she had turned the job down—Rupert would have expected a very good excuse; like she was dying, or her leg had fallen off.

She sighed, looking into the mirror. A thought struck her and her blood ran cold. Maybe Jake wanted a divorce. She shuddered, feeling suddenly very sick. But why? Wasn't that what she wanted? To get away from him for good, live a normal life? Suddenly, nothing was clear any more, and she rested her head in her hands, feeling miserable.

A knock on the door brought her head up, and she frowned. Was that Jake? Licking her lips nervously with her tongue, she called out, 'Who is it?' in a dry little voice.

The door opened, and Mike put his head round it. 'Hi!' he said cheerfully, running his eyes down over her, dressed in the fluffy towel. 'Oh, sorry—didn't know you were indecent.'

She laughed with relief. 'Very funny. What do you want?'

He raised his eyebrows. 'That's what's known as

a leading question,' he told her.

'Mike, stop being an idiot!' she admonished, watching him as he stood in the doorway.

He closed the door behind him and loped into the room. 'I wanted a chat. Don't worry, I won't try to seduce you unless you plead nicely,' he promised.

Laura sighed. 'Well, you're in now, so you might as well stay. But only for a minute. I'm not dressed, and I've got lots to do before dinner.' She took her dressing gown out of the wardrobe and stood, waiting for him to speak.

Mike leaned back on the bed, his arms folded behind his head as he gazed up at the ceiling. 'Steely character, Ashton, isn't he? I thought he was going to bite my head off when we first met.' He looked at her oddly. 'I wonder why?'

Laura shrugged. 'Maybe he got out of bed the wrong side. How should I know what was the matter with him?' How indeed, she thought to herself wryly.

Mike eyed her. 'Hmm,' he said. 'Still, he's not as bad as that Winterbottom woman—a most peculiar person if ever I saw one. She looked as if she wanted to slice me in two with a breadknife!'

Laura laughed. 'I suppose she grows on you.'

He raised an eyebrow. 'Like poison ivy.' He studied the ceiling again. 'Anyway, what I wanted to know was—which angle are you trying for on the interview? If you're going to give her a good wholesome write-up, I'll take good wholesome pictures. On the other hand, if you want her looking like Monroe,' he winked at her, 'I'm your man.'

She smiled. 'Didn't Rupert give you any idea at all?'

'Nope. He just patted me on the back and asked if I wanted more champagne.'

Her cheeks dimpled. 'Well, it's a bit early in the day to tell. I'll have to see how it goes.'

'But that could take centuries!' complained Mike.

She shrugged. 'Well, you'll just have to wait.'

He pulled a face. 'I'll get bored.'

'Well, play with your toes or something.'

He looked offended. 'Thanks! I'm not that bad. I do have my resources, you know.' He shrugged. 'I can nip down to the local and take some pictures of the gruesome regulars.'

'You just do that.' Laura hitched her towel up, worried that it might slip, tightening the knot between her breasts. 'But right now, I have to get dressed, so I'd be pleased if you'd go and play somewhere else.'

She heard a movement outside her door, and stopped talking, her eyes narrowing. Mike looked over at her, still lying on the bed. 'What's up?' he asked cheerfully.

The door opened, and Jake stood there, his hard face grim and forbidding, his eyes glittering.

Laura was frozen to the spot. 'Jake!' she managed to say through dry lips.

Mike looked round at him, then did a visible double-take from the dangerous look in those steely blue eyes. He leapt off the bed quickly, saying, 'Well, I'll see you later, Laura.' He backed from Jake as he walked past him, not taking his eyes off him for a moment.

The door closed behind him and Jake and Laura stood facing each other in a hostile silence.

'What the hell was he doing in here?' Jake asked tightly.

She stood where she was, her hands clamped by her

sides in case the bathtowel should fall from its careful position. 'He wanted to talk to me,' she said, forcing her voice to remain steady.

His upper lip moved in a cold sneer. 'Is that so?' he drawled, and Laura's blood ran cold.

'Yes,' she stammered, avoiding his gaze. 'He wanted to know which angle to get on the interview. He has to know before he takes the pictures, you see. . . .' She paused, looked up at him to see his reaction, then rushed on, the words stumbling over themselves. 'Otherwise he might get the wrong kind of shots, or waste a lot of time, and that wouldn't do anyone any good, would it?'

'So he came here to——' Jake paused, his eyes steely and mocking, ' "talk" to you about it, did he?'

Her hands clutched at each other. 'Yes. We've worked together on several other occasions. I know him quite well.'

Jake slid his hands into his tight-fitting dark blue trousers. 'You know him well,' he repeated, watching her through heavy lids. 'How well?'

Laura wetted her lips with her tongue, and watched as his glance followed the nervous little movement. She coloured, looking away. 'He's just a friend,' she said quietly, remembering suddenly that Jake had witnessed Mike's casual embrace from the lift alcove.

Her eyes flew to his face. What must he have thought when he came in here to find Mike in her room while she wore practically nothing!

'Just good friends,' Jake drawled mockingly. He moved two steps towards her, every line of his hard body threatening. 'He's very familiar for "just good friends", don't you think?'

She looked up a fraction of an inch. 'I've known him for a year,' she protested in a quiet voice.

There was a little silence, then Jake said tightly, 'A year.' He stood watching her with a face like carved granite, his legs apart, his hands thrust into his pockets below the tight-fitting waistcoat which moulded his lean waist superbly. 'Ever since we split up, in fact.'

Laura swallowed. She was treading on dangerous ground. 'Yes,' she said quietly, 'but I've only ever treated him as a friend. We just work together.'

Part of her wanted to make it clear that she had never been anything more than a friend to Mike, but another part of her warned her that to protest too much would only aggravate Jake's temper.

'Met him on the rebound?' Jake asked unpleasantly, 'or did you know him before the wedding?'

She looked down at her hands. 'I met him when I started work on *Style*,' she told him in the same quiet, subdued voice. She looked up again after a few moments, unable to stand the tense silence between them.

'And he's been visiting your bedroom ever since,' Jake drawled nastily, his eyes narrowed as he watched her.

Laura took a deep breath, controlling her temper which was rising fast in the face of his insults. She walked across to the door. 'I'm not going to discuss it with you any more, Jake. There's nothing between Mike and me.' She swallowed, seeing the dangerous glint in his eye. 'Would you please leave now? She opened the door and waited. 'I want to get dressed.'

He came over to the door with a grim, menacing face, his eyes glittering a dangerous blue. His hand pressed down on hers and he closed the door. 'You wouldn't want everyone to hear our conversation, would you?'

Her temper flared at the biting grip on her hand. 'Planning on shouting, are you?' she snapped, trying to pull her wrist out of his grasp as her bones pressed painfully against the door handle.

A cold smile curved his lips, and his hand tightened on hers. 'Is he your lover?' he asked in an icy voice.

Laura's eyes widened in shock, her face flooding with hot colour. 'Mind your own damned business!' she grated between her teeth before she could stop herself, anger exploding inside her at his blunt, calculatedly insulting remark.

Jake twisted her arm behind her back with a swift movement, smiling in an unpleasant way which made her spine tingle with fear. 'But it is my business, Laura,' he told her.' You're still my wife. If you choose to take lovers you must expect me to make it my business.'

Her lips tightened as her temper shot up. 'I'm not your wife any longer and you know it!' she hissed. 'You threw our marriage away a year ago, and you've got no right to come here asking me personal questions like this.'

'Perhaps not,' he said tightly, 'but that makes no difference. If you're sleeping with that curly-headed idiot I intend to find out about it.'

Her eyes flashed a bright angry green. 'I've told you,' she snapped, frightened by his mood, 'he's just a friend.'

Jake shook his head. 'No dice, Laura. I don't believe you.'

There was a very tense silence. Laura could hear nothing but her own laboured breathing, her thudding heartbeat as she stared up at Jake.

He smiled down at her unpleasantly, his hand tightening, making her wince. 'Is he good in bed?' he drawled icily.

She flushed, her mouth tightening into an angry line. 'Get out of here!' she forced the words out between clenched teeth.

His smile grew savage. 'I don't know what you see in him. He's not your type.'

She was breathing deeply, her temper red-hot. 'And just what is my type?' she asked.

His eyes glittered mockingly. 'I am.'

His arrogance took her breath away. 'Don't flatter yourself!' she spat, her back arched like an angry kitten. 'I wouldn't touch you if you went down on your knees and begged me to!'

There was a glimpse of manic fury in his face. 'Wouldn't you?' he said bitingly, his eyes pinning her against the door. He moved closer, his hand taking her other wrist, clamping both arms above her head, pressing her against the door while she struggled bitterly.

'Don't touch me!' she whispered, knowing it would do her no good.

Jake smiled cruelly, his gaze dropping to the knot in the towel just above her breasts. He moved his hand to the knot, holding it there, one long finger stroking the hollow between her breasts.

His gaze returned to her eyes. 'Your heart's going like a steam hammer,' he observed, and Laura swallowed on a tight throat, feeling the thud of her heart hammering through her body, her breathing laboured as her breasts moved quickly, brushing against the silk of his waistcoat.

'Do I excite you, Laura?' he asked thickly, his eyes burning with sexuality.

She felt her breath catch in her throat, feeling the shock waves of sexual arousal flood through her with a heat that threatened to make her go crazy. 'No,' she whispered through dry lips.

The blue eyes were riveted on her. 'Liar,' he said thickly, his black head swooping down quickly.

His hands moved from her wrists, letting her arms go free. He gripped her shoulders ruthlessly, his hands biting into her flesh as he pulled her towards him. Her heart fluttered wildly in her chest, her breathing laboured as fear set in.

The kiss was brutal, punishing, his mouth moving harshly over hers, forcing her lips back until she tasted the salty flow of blood on her tongue. She struggled, trying to put her hands up to his chest to push him away, but he was too strong, too angry to be halted.

His hands left her shoulders, moving to her back as he pressed her hard against him, until she could feel every muscle, every line of that hard, lithe body.

Hot tears pricked against her eyes as his arms tightened around her, hurting her, like steel bands as they kept her prisoner. His lips were hurting her, hard and ruthless as they punished the soft skin of her mouth. She tried to twist her head away, but one hand came back to clamp her face in position.

Suddenly the kiss changed. His hands softened on her, his mouth moving less harshly, becoming teasing, sensuous. She felt the change from deep within her as she moaned in the back of her throat and began to respond.

Jake's warm mouth moved sensuously over hers, his

hands sliding down her back, making her shiver from her head right down to her toes. She wound her arms round his neck, tangling her fingers in the thick black hair, pressing herself warmly against him.

She felt the towel slip away, leaving her naked skin shivering with pleasure as those long fingers slid over her, igniting fires where they touched. She was breathing harshly, her heart pounding.

Excitement mingled with fear as her blood pressure shot up, leaving her shaking as she stroked his face, her fingertips trembling on the tanned skin. His mouth left hers, moving down to her throat.

She groaned as she felt his tongue snake out across her neck, his breath fanning her skin, making her tingle with heat. She sought and found his mouth eagerly, and passion flared between them with the power of a huge flame roaring inside both of them.

The long fingers slid slowly, sensually down her back, moving round to glide across her hips, caressing them, pulling her further against him. Her breath caught in her throat, and she arched herself towards him, ignoring the warning protests going off in her head.

His hands slid to her thighs, and she felt the exquisite, searing heat melt her limbs, her mouth moving with heated urgency, her heart hammering inside her, her mind oblivious to everything except this hot, sweet, urgent desire.

Jake's hands began to move upwards, along the flat planes of her stomach, moving slowly, tantalisingly towards her smooth breasts. She ached for his touch, her breath coming faster as she tried and failed to hold her breath, arching herself towards him, needing to feel his hands on her.

The strong brown hands cupped her breasts and she moaned, a sound from deep in her throat as he caressed them, running one long finger over her hard pink nipple.

'Laura,' he muttered hoarsely, looking down at her with eyes that blazed like glowing coals. 'I need you, I still need you.'

She watched with glazed eyes as the black head bent to her breasts, and waited, her breath hurting in her chest. His tongue snaked out across her nipple, and she gasped, envisaging her breast as a burning hot fruit, ripe for his touch, throbbing as she waited for his touch. She pressed his head closer to her, her fingers tightening in his hair.

'Oh God,' he muttered in a voice raw with emotion, 'you're so beautiful.'

He lifted his head, his gaze skimming over her naked body as she heard his breath catch in the back of his throat. His mouth swooped down on hers again, demanding, insistent, hungry as he ran urgent fingers along her naked skin, stroking her waist, her hips, her thighs, roaming her body with heated, sensuous movements.

She pressed her trembling hands against the hard wall of his chest, touching, stroking, feeling, as she slipped one hand inside his shirt, groaning as her palm made contact with the hot, smooth brown flesh.

His heart was crashing manically against his rib cage, his breathing coming in raw gasps as he kissed her, pressing her closer to him, his hands becoming more urgent.

He made a strangled noise in the back of his throat. 'Oh yes,' he said thickly, his hands sliding down her legs to her knees as he swung her into his arms, carrying her over to the bed and laying her on it gently, her long golden body stretched out invitingly, her skin glowing like a ripe peach.

Laura watched through a golden haze as he slipped out of his jacket, unbuttoning the white shirt with trembling fingers. A sensuous smile curved her lips as her eyes focussed on the smooth brown chest, the powerful shoulders. She needed to feel those strong brown arms holding her, crushing her against him, making her feel safe and warm and fulfilled.

Then his mouth swooped down to her again, making her blood rush up to her head, her heart pounding in a hot, heavy rhythm filled with deep, honeyed excitement. She met his kiss with her own, holding him to her as his hands ran urgently up and down her thighs, making her gasp in undisguised pleasure.

Her body was on fire as she wrapped herself around him, drawing him closer, meeting the driving, sensual movements with the same heated urgency until her body spiralled up into a taut, exquisite pleasure.

'Sweet,' he murmured thickly against her ear as they moved as one, 'you're so sweet. You're so, so sweet.'

Laura arched herself against him with a gasping breath as shivers drove through her, her breath forced out of her in hot, frenzied gasps, her body moving against him in quick, sharp excitement, leaving her breathless, dizzy, totally fulfilled.

Jake's release came soon after, his voice calling her name hoarsely as he drove against her, his fingers biting into her. She watched his tanned, attractive face through hazy eyes, seeing his brows pulled in a frown of exquisite pleasure, his mouth slightly open, exposing even white teeth as the breath was forced out of him.

Later, Laura lay in the circle of his arms, feeling confused, guilty, unsure and anxious. His strong hand stroked her hair, twining the long red-gold strands in his fingers.

They lay in silence, each unsure of what to say to the other. It had happened so quickly, so unexpectedly. They had built up to far worse arguments in the past, but none had culminated in lovemaking. Laura bit her lip deeply. They had never been in a bedroom alone together before since their wedding day.

Jake was the first to speak. 'Are you all right?' he asked deeply, stroking her cheek tenderly with one long finger.

She nodded, staring at his chest. 'Yes,' she replied in a husky whisper.

She listened to his breathing, her head against his chest, feeling the heavy thud of his heartbeat as it slowed gradually, matching the warm thud of her own. She felt sweet and warm, her body glowing with something she found hard to describe. She frowned, trying to analyse her feelings for him.

Obviously, she was still in love with him. No woman could respond so urgently to a man without feeling more for him than physical attraction. Their lovemaking had been insistent, urgent, but at the same time tinged with a sweet inevitability, as though she had been running away from destiny for too long. She smiled sadly. Perhaps she was getting morbid now. Or perhaps it was just that all women felt the same little sadness after lovemaking.

Women are strange creatures, she thought with a

frown. We seem to have a fountain of emotions, stored up to be released at a certain time, a certain place. Jake had released those feelings for her. She had never felt such a deep, all-consuming love for anyone before. Now, it flowed over her like a wave, leaving her unable to think of any future, any life, without Jake.

A knock on the door brought both of them out of their separate thoughts, and she glanced at Jake worriedly.

'Ask who it is,' Jake whispered, kissing her forehead with gentle lips.

She sat up a little, without moving out of the circle of his arms. 'Who is it?' she called shakily.

'Me,' said a voice.

'It's Theresa,' Jake whispered, frowning, his arms tightening around Laura.

Laura looked at him, horrified. 'What shall I say?' she whispered worriedly.

He hesitated. 'Tell her you're getting dressed.'

She looked back at the door, pulling the sheet tightly around her. 'I'm getting dressed. Was it anything important?'

'Oh.' Theresa's voice came through the door again. 'Well, I was looking for Jake. He appears to have disappeared. Last time he was heard of, he was coming up here to talk to you about the interview. Have you seen him?'

Laura looked at Jake. He shook his head.

'No.' Laura called back. 'Maybe he's gone out.'

There was a little silence, then Theresa said in a very unconvinced voice, 'Oh.' She paused. 'Oh, well, all right. I'll go and hunt him out. Someone just rang, you see, and I've got to deliver a message.'

'Well, I'll tell him you're looking for him if he does come up,' Laura said hopefully, wishing she would go away.

'Right.' Theresa sounded disbelieving. 'Okay, I'll see you at dinner, then.'

She moved off down the corridor, and Laura sank back into Jake's arms with a sigh.

Jake stroked her hair, dropping a kiss on her forehead. 'That was close,' he murmured, a smile in his voice.

Laura stroked his hand tenderly. 'Mmm. I wonder who it was who rang for you,' she said, thinking out loud.

Jake kissed her again. 'I'd better go and see,' he said gently.

Laura stiffened. She didn't want him to leave her side. 'Do you have to?' she asked huskily.

He sighed. 'It could be important. If Theresa comes back, she might come in this time. You wouldn't spend half an hour getting dressed, now would you?'

Laura frowned. 'But I told her you might have gone out.'

He gave her an amused smile. 'How can I be out if my car is still here?' he pointed out.

Laura gave a disappointed sigh. 'Oh yes.'

He kissed her again, sliding out of the bed and getting dressed while she watched him. When he was dressed, he leaned over and dropped a light kiss on her nose.

'I shouldn't be long. I'll come back up here as soon as I can. We have a lot of talking to do.'

Laura lay in silence when he had gone, remembering every kiss, every caress until she felt the warmth begin again inside her. A smile curved her lips, and she waited for Jake to return.

CHAPTER SEVEN

But Jake did not return that afternoon. In fact, he didn't arrive back at the house until long after Laura had gone to bed. She had listened to the sound of his car pulling up outside, the slam of the door, the crunch of his footsteps as he walked up the gravel path to the front door.

She had lain still, not daring to breathe, as her door had opened, and a shaft of light flooded through into the darkness.

'Laura?' Jake had asked quietly. 'Are you awake?'

She had ignored him, her eyes shut tightly, lying in a tense silence. He had left the room a moment later, and she had breathed out with relief, turning on her side, her face buried in the pillow as she cried great, wrenching tears of betrayal.

The next morning, she had been woken up by long golden fingers of sunlight which crept through the window, touching her lids, stroking her into arousal. She had smelt the crisp, morning dew mingling with the early morning sunshine and had felt a need to get up and go out into the garden.

It was even more beautiful at this time of day than she had suspected it would be, and she wandered along the green lawns, looking at the rows of dancing rose bushes, her face pensive, as she thought of the previous evening. Dinner had been an ordeal for her. Jake's empty chair had tugged at her heart and her pride, while Russ Taylor and his wife Theresa had kept up the conversation, their bubbly conversation spilling out on to everyone, so that those who wished to join in had only to speak up.

A footstep behind her startled her, and she whirled, expecting to see Jake behind her.

'Hullo, hullo,' said a lazy sophisticated voice as she turned, 'what have we here? I didn't know we had fairies in the bottom of our garden. Or are you a woodland nymph?'

She smiled. It was Russ Taylor. He looked like a handsome, decadent gypsy, his black curly hair falling to brush his shoulders, a gold earring in his left ear, his black eyes incredibly wicked-looking as they wandered over her.

'Good morning, Mr Taylor,' she said, feeling relieved. Russ Taylor presented no problems. He was a fun-loving very lighthearted man who wanted only to be loved and admired by all around him.

He gave her a reproachful look. 'Mr Taylor?' one wicked brow surged upwards. 'How very proper. You called me Russ last night, if I remember rightly. Not getting formal on me, I hope?'

She smiled again, genuinely amused. She knew his flirtatious ways were meant to be taken lightly. That was their charm, they were paid to every woman who came within an inch of Mr Russ Taylor, and they served only to make women happy. Laura didn't mind being happy.

'Like my garden, do you?' he asked as they began to walk back towards the house at a slow pace.

She nodded, turning her vivid head to smile at him. 'It's beautiful. You must work very hard to keep it in this condition.'

He gave a sigh. 'Ah, I must confess, it is not I who keeps this garden as lovely as it is.' He grinned. 'It's all down to Gaston, the gardener. He comes in most mornings and potters around, muttering in French, throwing up his hands and wailing in despair.'

Laura laughed. 'He sounds like fun.'

'Oh, he's a real bundle of laughs,' said Russ, moving over to another rose bush. He leaned over and plucked a long-stemmed pink rose. 'Here,' he said, handing it to her, 'have a rose.'

She took it, smiling, lifting it to her face and inhaling the delicate scent. 'Why, thank you,' she murmured.

Russ leaned over to pick another rose, but jumped back as his finger encountered another thorn. He examined the tip of his finger, frowning as he saw the tiny pin-prick of blood. 'Just like women,' he commented, sucking his finger. 'Soft and beautiful on top, but when you get down to the nitty-gritty, there's always a thorn somewhere.'

Laura slid him a teasing glance. 'Well, don't say you haven't been warned.'

They started walking again, and Laura found herself thinking about Jake. He had been so tender towards her when he left her side. He had promised to return as quickly as he could. So where had he got to? She bit her lip. Perhaps something really important had come up and he had had to rush off somewhere. Had she been too harsh in her judgment? She wondered whether or not she should have spoken to him when he came to her room the previous night. Then she shrugged. She would wait and see. There would be plenty of opportunities for him to tell her exactly what had happened.

'So how long are you here for?' Russ's cheerful voice broke into her thoughts. 'I know Jake said he'd be staying for around a week, but then,' his eyes flashed wickedly over her and he grinned, 'you ain't Jake.'

She laughed, her cheeks dimpling. 'I don't know. It all depends on how fast the interview gets done. But it'll probably be for around a week, yes.'

'Really?' He sounded pleased. 'Sounds like fun. We could get to know each other pretty well in a week.'

'On the other hand. . . .' Laura murmured drily, her green eyes amused as they slid sideways to look at him.

'Well, that's not nice, is it?' he admonished, laughing. 'You're a rotten spoilsport—give me back my rose.'

'No,' she said, holding back a smile as she pulled it out of his reach. 'I'm going to put it in a vase. It'll brighten up my room.'

Russ sighed exaggeratedly. 'I knew it! Beneath that charming exterior beats a heart of reinforced concrete.' He whistled under his breath as they walked, his face cheerful and trouble-free. Then he looked back at her with a smile. 'Are you going to interview me too? Or do I get fobbed off with Jenson? I'd much rather you did the interview,' he pleaded nicely.

'I'm here to interview both of you,' she told him.

He grinned. 'Wonderful! I knew we were going to get along the minute I saw your lovely face. We'll have to take a whole day out for the interview—just you and me locked up in a little room somewhere.'

Laura shook her head gravely. 'The idea doesn't appeal somehow.'

He put the rose between his teeth. 'We could always tango afterwards,' he suggested.

She laughed, 'You're worse than Mike. The pair of you are idiots!'

He held up his hands in defeat. 'Okay, okay, you win! I know when I'm beaten.' They walked further and Russ asked, 'If I said I'd never heard of you professionally before, would you be offended?'

'Not really,' she shrugged. 'I wouldn't be in the least bit surprised. This is my first break.' Her lips tightened as she remembered that she hadn't really earned it—Jake had thrust it to her on a silver platter.

Russ gave her an odd glance. 'Strange they should send such an inexperienced reporter. I suppose you just shot up out of nowhere?'

She made light of his comment. 'Do I look like a beanstalk?'

'A beanstalk with possibilities,' he said, eyeing her.

They reached the edge of the driveway just as a sleek red sports car pulled up, tyres screeching, gravel thrown up by the wheels. Russ frowned, and they both walked to the front door. A woman stepped out of the car, standing tall and graceful. She looked straight at Laura.

Laura's heart kicked painfully in her chest as she stared in numb disbelief at the woman.

Melissa Blake's face still held that wild beauty, her enormous tragic blue eyes were set in a face which was almost chalk-white, her lips a natural deep red, her face frail and delicate. Long silky black hair tumbled over her shoulders.

'Melissa!' Russ was smiling and holding out his hands to her. 'My exquisite little angel! I didn't know you were coming over. I didn't expect you until at least Friday.'

Melissa was still staring at Laura, a mixture of sorrow and anxiety in the haunted blue eyes. 'I rang Theresa,' she said, her voice soft, 'and she said she'd tell you.'

Russ grinned. 'Typical! She's got a face like an angel, but a mind like a sieve.'

There was a little silence. Laura felt numb and stiff. The first shock of seeing Melissa after all this time was gradually wearing off. What was she doing here? Had Jake invited her?

'Melissa,' Russ took her delicate white hand and led her to the entrance where Laura stood, 'I'd like you to meet the lady with the thousand pencils behind her ear—our friendly neighbourhood reporter, Laura Hadleigh. Laura, this, as you might have gathered, is Melissa—model extraordinaire.'

They stared at each other for a moment, each uncertain of how to react, how to handle the situation. Then Melissa offered a tentative hand.

'Hello, Miss Hadleigh,' she said quietly, her voice soft and gentle.

Laura shook her hand stiffly. 'Miss Blake,' she managed to say as politely as she could.

Melissa smiled rather uncertainly. 'Actually, it's Mrs Radcliffe,' she said, 'but I'd rather you called me Melissa,' and the luminous blue eyes searched Laura's face for some flicker of emotion.

Mrs Radcliffe? Laura thought, frowning. But when had she got married? It couldn't have been long ago,

unless she had already been married when she knew
Jake.

Russ was watching her with a frown. He had obviously picked up the uncertainty between her and
Melissa, the sorrow in Melissa's eyes. 'Why don't we
all go inside?' he suggested slowly, his eyes on Laura
as he tried to read her mind. 'I don't know about you,
but I could do with some coffee.'

Laura gave him a polite smile. 'Why not?'

Russ looked at her oddly, then walked into the house
saying, 'I don't think Terry's up yet. She looked a bit
dead last time I poked my head round the door, but
you never know, she might have got up—stranger
things have been known to happen.'

Melissa watched Laura with those enormous blue
eyes and Laura found herself becoming even more
tense. What was the woman doing here?

'Mrs Winterbottom!' Russ called as he turned into
the morning room. 'Coffee for three in here!'

There was a loud crash from the kitchen, which Russ
noted with a smile. He gestured towards the wicker
chairs positioned around a square wicker table. 'Sit
down. We always have breakfast in here because the
sun comes in the windows. Well, I always have breakfast here—Theresa can't because she's too busy staying
slim and beautiful, poor soul.'

Mrs Winterbottom bustled in with a large tray and a
cross expression. She gave Laura a nasty smile. 'You're
up early and no mistake. I thought all you journalist
types stayed in bed till all hours.' She grinned malici-
ously. 'Mr Russell always says you're a lazy bunch
of. . . .'

'Thank you, Mrs Winterbottom!' Russ cut in

hurriedly, giving the woman a warning glance.

She went out of the room with a sniff, giving Laura another nasty smile as she went.

Russ grinned at Laura sheepishly. 'I don't know why Terry insisted on dragging her over here from Yorkshire. She's a poisonous old bat at the best of times. But she worked for Terry's family for years apparently, and she's so sweet, how could I refuse?' he winked. 'Terry, that is. Mrs Winterbottom's about as sweet as a rhinoceros.'

They sipped their coffee while Russ kept the conversation going. The obvious silence between Laura and Melissa was becoming embarrassing, and she knew Russ had noticed it, because he kept giving her odd little glances from time to time, enquiry in his eyes, curiosity knitted into his frown.

Laura felt uncomfortable, but at the same time she felt bitterly angry with Jake. What was Melissa doing here? Had Jake invited her here? She had never really met or been introduced to Melissa, but she had never forgotten that beautiful, delicate, haunting face. It had been with her for the past year, frozen into her brain with painful clarity.

'I'll give her a shout in a minute,' Russ was saying, 'but I warn you, she's like nothing on earth before ten o'clock.'

'Don't worry,' Melissa said softly, 'I'll wait until she wakes up.'

Laura glanced at her, her lips tightening. Nobody had the right to be that beautiful, she thought, her heart constricting. Melissa looked like a latter-day Cathy Earnshaw. And Jake Ashton is her Heathcliff, Laura thought, staring miserably into her coffee cup.

'Laura's here to do an interview with me and Terry,' Russ told Melissa, 'She's as sharp as a knife, unfortunately. I think she's planning to rip us to shreds with her nasty little claws. Am I right, lovely?' He looked at Laura with wicked black eyes.

Laura looked up, forcing her emotions under control. 'I've been warned to be as nice as pie,' she said with a sweet smile.

Russ laughed. 'I was worrying for nothing. She's going to pin haloes on us!'

Melissa smiled gently at Laura, her luminous blue eyes kind. 'I'm sure she'll do a good job.'

Laura averted her eyes. Why did Melissa have to be so nice? It was pretty difficult to hate someone if they looked at you with eyes like an angel and spoke to you like a nun. She ground her teeth silently. If it weren't for the recurring nightmare of seeing Melissa lying on that bed with Jake, she would probably end up liking the woman very much indeed.

The door opened suddenly, and Laura tensed, feeling the hair on the back of her neck prickle with awareness. She knew it was Jake, even before anyone spoke or moved.

'Good morning,' he said in that deep, smoky voice as he closed the door behind him.

Melissa looked at him and smiled softly. 'Hello, Jake.'

He leant over, brushing his hard mouth against her cheek with a warm smile. 'I'm glad you could make it,' he said, straightening. 'It's good to see you again.'

Laura stared broodingly at the floor.

'Thank you. I came as soon as I could,' Melissa replied in a gentle voice.

Russ was watching this with great curiosity. 'So it was you who invited her out here,' he said with a grin. 'I did wonder.'

So did I, thought Laura, her lips tight, and now I know it doesn't make it any better.

Jake's eyes rested on her bent head for a brief second, but she ignored them. 'Yes,' he replied, moving to take a seat around the table, sitting next to Laura, much to her further discomfort. 'How's Peter?' he asked Melissa.

She smiled, her eyes filled with a new sparkle. 'He's very well,' she said in a voice which seemed to have brightened considerably, and there was a warmth behind her words that made Laura frown. Was Peter her husband? If so, why was she here? Surely Jake had called her over because he wanted her here as his mistress? She could think of no other explanation.

Melissa sipped her coffee and continued. 'He said he'd fly out here in a few days,' she told them, her voice filled with warmth. 'He wants to get here in time for the party.'

Jake nodded, his smile warm. He looked at Russ. 'Theresa not around yet?' he enquired.

Russ shook his head. 'Nope. Neither is that photographer fellow. I suppose he's pottering about somewhere, although I haven't seen hide nor hair of him since earlier this morning.'

Jake leaned over, lifting up the lid of the coffee pot with one long tanned hand. 'Any left?' he asked as he did so.

'Should be.' Russ peered at it. 'Just enough for one cup. She always makes too much in case anyone wants some more.'

Jake poured himself some coffee while Laura's eyes strayed over him. He looked sexy this morning, very sexy, dressed in black jeans which moulded the length of his legs, the narrow waist and hips, and a black cashmere sweater that was beautifully cut, emphasising the power and muscular strength of his hard chest and shoulders.

Russ put his cup on the table. 'Well, if you'll all excuse me, I'd better go and yank Her Majesty out of bed. She'll only get cross if I don't—you know how she loves to see you, Melissa.' He walked to the door and left the room.

Please don't go, thought Laura desperately, but it was too late. The door closed behind him and silence descended like a malevolent cloud. She stared, apparently riveted by her empty cup, feeling the tension make her hair stand on end. Why had Jake done this? He must have known how deeply he would hit at her with it, how angry she would be.

It was so stupid, she thought as the silence lengthened. They all knew what had happened between them, yet they were sitting in here, politely, not speaking, almost as though they barely knew one another. Their lives, however, had been woven together by an unbreakable, invisible thread, holding all of them captive, hurting all of them in its own way.

Suddenly she couldn't stand it any more. She stood up, pushing her chair back with a shaky hand. 'I've got work to do,' she said tightly.

Jake stood up, towering over her, looking down at her with heavy-lidded eyes. 'I want you to stay for a while, Laura,' he said slowly. 'I want you to talk to Melissa.'

She swallowed. 'Talk?' she asked with false brightness. 'What about?'

He watched her enigmatically. 'I asked Melissa to come down here because I think you should talk to her. It's not just a whim of mine, it's very important.'

Laura's hands clenched into tight fists. 'Important? Important to whom?'

He surveyed her. 'To both of us—all of us.'

Melissa spoke in a soft, almost inaudible voice. 'Yes, Laura. I think you should listen to what I have to say. It should have been said a long time ago, only you never gave either of us the chance.'

Her eyes flashed bright green. 'Is that so? Well, let me tell you something amidst all this great importance. I don't think you have anything to say that is either important or even worth listening to.'

Melissa watched her with great compassion, a frown of pain marring her forehead, sorrow and anxiety in those haunted blue eyes. 'Please, Laura, don't be so angry. It could all be sorted out if you would stop and listen.' Her voice was soft but with an inner core of strength to it.

Laura eyed her bitterly. She could see the pity on her face, hear it in her voice. Her temper began to rise higher. She couldn't bear pity. 'I didn't ask you to come here,' she said angrily. 'I didn't ask to speak to you. Why don't you just go back where you came from and leave me alone?'

Jake took her hand. 'Laura, I asked Melissa to come here. You mustn't blame her.'

'Oh no, I'm not allowed to blame anyone, am I? Everything that happens around here is my fault. Well, you can both just disappear down a great black hole for all I care! I don't care why you brought her here, and I don't want you to tell me either—I'm not interested in the sordid details of your love life!'

His hand tightened on her wrist. 'You're on the wrong track, Laura,' he said tightly.

She pulled her wrist out of his grasp. 'Oh, of course, I would be. I've got a mind like a sewer. But you haven't, have you? You're as pure as the driven snow.'

Jake pushed his hands into the pockets of his black jeans, watching her with eyes that flashed with the beginning of anger. 'I know what you're thinking, but you're wrong. There's absolutely nothing between Melissa and myself but friendship.'

She flung him a blistering smile. 'I believe you,' she said sarcastically. 'Thousands wouldn't.'

His mouth firmed into an angry line. 'If she was more than a friend, I would hardly bring her down here to meet you, would I? Use your head, Laura. Stop thinking of the present alongside the past.'

Her face tightened angrily. He was too damned clever to play word games with. He would hold up your faults in order to make you believe you were wrong. He picked on anything, however small, so long as it won him a point in the argument.

'Frankly,' said Laura between her teeth, 'nothing you did would surprise me. You're very good at hiding your motives. How should I know what twisted little plot you've hatched up there?' She gestured at his smooth black head.

Jake's face darkened, filled with restrained anger. 'Melissa and I were involved with each other once, but that was all over a long time ago. It was over the minute I met you.'

'How very convenient!' Laura snapped, turning away from him. She couldn't bear to look at either of them any more.

Melissa stood up slowly, standing behind Laura as she spoke, her voice filled with sadness. 'He's telling the truth, Laura,' she said quietly. 'I didn't know it at the time, but it was all over the minute he set eyes on you. It wasn't his fault.' She glanced at Jake with a sad smile. 'He couldn't help himself. He fell for you so quickly—neither of us could have predicted it.'

Laura felt her lips trembling—whether it was from pain or anger she couldn't be sure. All she knew was that she had to get out of that room—fast.

Jake touched her shoulder with one strong hand. 'Will you sit down and listen now?' he asked in a deep smoky voice.

She turned round slowly, her eyes bright with anger and unshed tears. 'Sorry, Mrs Radcliffe, but I don't think I can stand the sight of you for much longer,' she said in a high voice.

Jake's eyes flashed. 'Don't be so bloody rude,' he said tightly. 'Sit down and listen.'

She pushed his hand away from her shoulder. 'Get your hands off me! I've had enough of you,' she glared bitterly at Melissa, 'and you. The pair of you make me sick! You couldn't wait five minutes to get your hands on each other, could you? You destroyed my wedding day, messed up my life, and went off without a thought about me. You forgot I even existed until now.'

'That's a lie!' Jake bit out, his eyes blazing with anger.

'It's the truth,' she hissed. 'You didn't even re-member I was alive until we met in that nightclub, did you? Well, you can go to hell for all I care, both of you!'

The door opened suddenly, and they all froze as they were, their expressions almost comical as Mike Jenson wandered into the room, scratching his curly head with a bony finger.

Laura broke out of her trance first, and ran out of the door, pushing past Mike as she scrambled up the stairs to her room.

'What's up with her?' Mike's voice floated up the stairs as she ran. 'Have I suddenly developed leprosy or something?'

She was breathing hard when she reached her room. She slammed the door behind her and leaned on it, her eyes closed as she forced the hot tears to stay where they were.

How dared he bring that woman here to patronise her? That soft, tragic voice made her want to throw up. She was so sweet and good, almost unreal. Melissa made her feel sick. Every time she looked at her she saw that tableau, Jake by her side, his hair tousled, Melissa's face glowing, her lips bruised, her hair in disarray.

How could they deny it? Surely they realised that she would never ever believe that they hadn't been lovers? She sighed shaking her head. Jake was so obstinate. She knew he wasn't going to give up on this without a fight.

A frown marred her forehead. Why wouldn't he give up? What was so important to him that he kept trying to make her believe it? She bit her lip. Surely he didn't still feel something for her?

Her heart leapt on a wild surge of feeling, and she

twisted her hands together, biting her lower lip anxiously. Why did she still feel so much for him? After all the pain, the agony he had caused her, why did the thought that he might still feel something for her make her want to dance and sing and run around in joyous circles?

I'm a fool, she thought bitterly. A stupid, prideless, idiotic little fool. After all this time, and all this pain, I'm still in love with the man. She sighed. Why was it that one could never lose a feeling as deep as her love for Jake?

Love clings on to you with painful fingers. But Laura didn't want it to. She wanted to be able to feel indifference to Jake. She wanted to be able to walk away unconcerned from his touch, his voice and his presence. Instead, every time he was near she felt her body tingle with awareness and feeling. It was all so pointless, so stupid.

He's a heartless devil, she thought bitterly, and I'm still in love with him. She wanted to kick herself.

There was a knock on her door, and she jumped, her heart stopping with fear for a split second. She gripped the coverlet on the bed with a tight fist. Who was it? Jake? Melissa? She laughed inside with mild hysteria. There were so many people in this house, and they all seemed to visit her room. It was becoming worse than Euston Station!

'Laura? Are you in there?' It was Jake's voice which boomed through the door.

She stood up, her heart in her mouth, and tiptoed over to the bathroom, hiding in there and closing the door silently behind her.

The door clicked open, and she held her breath,

listening intently to the sound of his footsteps as he came into the bedroom.

'Laura?' His voice was crisp, no longer angry. She heard him moving around the room, and she squeezed herself up against the wall behind the door, praying that he wouldn't find her.

'Laura?' His voice was closer now, and she watched as the bathroom door swung open until it was only a few inches from her nose.

She bit her lip, holding her breath. Jake walked into the bathroom, looking around himself for a moment.

'Are you there?'

Please, go away, Laura thought desperately, biting deep into her lower lip as she tried to keep silent. Then the door swung back to reveal her, and she looked into a pair of angry blue eyes.

She swallowed. 'Hullo,' she said weakly.

He took her wrist and dragged her out of the bathroom, making her sit down on the bed while he towered over her. 'Why were you hiding in there?' he asked.

'It was more original than the wardrobe,' she replied tartly.

The blue eyes narrowed on her. 'Very funny!'

She glared at him. 'Well, why do you think I was hiding in there? I didn't want to see you—I still don't. But that doesn't make any difference to you, does it? You still come barging in here, forcing yourself on me!'

He took a deep breath, choosing his words carefully. 'I told you yesterday before I went—we still have a lot of talking to do.'

'Yes,' she snapped, feeling bitter. 'That was before you went. Where did you go, I wonder? Was it some great big complicated business deal—or was it something to do with our mutual friend downstairs?'

Jake watched her through heavy lids, his face controlled as he waited for her to finish speaking. 'I had to drive to Paris,' he said abruptly.

Laura raised her brows. 'You surprise me.' Her voice was sarcastic. 'That's where all the airports are, aren't they? In Paris, I mean. Melissa wasn't in Paris last night by any chance, was she?'

He slid his hands into his pockets. 'Yes, she was. She flew in yesterday from London.'

Laura gave him a blistering smile. 'And you went to meet her from the airport. How sweet!'

'Yes,' he said curtly.

'I suppose you had to show her how to get down here, did you?'

'She hasn't driven here on her own before, Laura. She might have got lost. Peter usually drives her.'

Laura glared at him. 'Well, why didn't you just stay the night in a hotel with her and drive her down in the morning? That would have killed two birds with one stone, wouldn't it?'

His face tightened with anger, but he controlled it, his heavy lids dropping over the blue eyes to hide the expression in them from her. 'Laura, I've told you, she is not my mistress.'

Laura tried to keep her cool. She looked at him with barely veiled contempt, her brows raised with cold hauteur. 'No? Well, perhaps not any more. But don't forget—I saw you lying on a bed with her, so there must have been something in it.'

Jake took another deep breath, his face brooding, dark. 'I can see you're obviously upset, Laura. . . .'

'Damned right I am!' she snapped, her eyes flashing

a bright angry green as she interrupted him. 'You took me to bed yesterday afternoon, then you jumped up the minute you'd finished making love to me and ran off to Paris to be with another woman—the same woman you were seeing when we married a year ago. Do you blame me for being angry?'

A deep tide of red washed up over his face, and the blue eyes flashed with an emotion which she could not decipher. 'There's no point in talking to you when you're in this sort of mood, Laura. I'll leave it till later.'

'I don't want you to leave it till later! I don't want to hear it—and that means ever!' She stood up while she spoke, facing him with bitter anger, hurt pride shining out of her eyes.

He watched her for a moment in silence, the expression on his face hovering dangerously between anger and self-control. 'I've waited a year,' he said tightly, 'I suppose I can wait a little longer.'

He turned on his heel and left her room, closing the door quietly behind him. Laura bit her lip, walking over to the window and gazing out on the gardens below. It was so peaceful out there, so tranquil. Why can't my brain be peaceful and tranquil? she thought with a sigh.

She wandered downstairs in time for lunch, looking around herself carefully as she went, wondering whether Jake was about too. She went into the dining room, her eyes darting around as she searched for Jake, but there was no sign of him.

Theresa greeted her with a wide friendly smile. 'Hi there! Had a good morning?' she bubbled around the room, her long blonde hair giving her the appearance of an over-excited sunbeam. 'I've only been up for two hours or so. I felt ghastly when I surfaced. Russ came and bounced me out of bed while I was still in the land of nod. Did you meet my friend Melissa? Lovely, isn't she? It's not fair—I don't stand a chance when she's around, but I can't help liking her, she's so sweet.'

Laura let this pour over her ears while she smiled and moved further into the room. Russ lounged by the drinks cabinet in the corner, dressed in black trousers and an outrageous bright pink jacket.

'Hello, lovely,' he said, adjusting the white carnation in the buttonhole of the pink jacket. 'Like a drink?'

'Martini, please.' Laura walked over to take the glass he offered her a moment later. 'Where is everyone?' she enquired.

Theresa waved a benign hand. 'Oh, Mike's gone wandering off into the village to snap the local yokels. He says you'd know all about that.'

Laura stifled a smile. Mike appeared to have a soft spot for anyone who was either young and vibrantly beautiful or old and wrinkled. He said they always made the best shots, and he was probably right, because he took some very good photos.

'And Jake's taken Melissa out for lunch up the road,' Theresa continued.

Laura's head swung round a little too quickly. 'Oh?' she said, frowning.

Russ was watching her closely, his black eyes shrewd. 'That's what they told us. They had to go out to do some shopping for Melissa, and they decided to stop off and have lunch somewhere.'

Laura accepted this with a calm face, masking the

turbulent emotions running inside her. 'So they won't be back for a couple of hours,' she commented, trying to make polite conversation.

Russ shrugged. 'They didn't say, but I shouldn't imagine so. They're old friends.' He paused, watching her reaction. 'But then you know that, don't you?'

Laura sipped her drink. 'Mike's not coming back to lunch then either?' she asked casually.

Russ grinned, admiring the deft change of subject. 'No,' he drawled, 'Mike's not coming back to lunch. It's just us and Mrs Winterbottom all alone in the house.' He gave her a fiendish grin.

They had lunch in the dining room overlooking the pond outside. Theresa and Russ kept the conversation going, while Laura merely toyed with her food. So much for all Jake's protestations, she thought angrily. He had taken her out to lunch in some beautiful French restaurant, leaving Laura alone here.

In the afternoon, Laura stayed in her room, trying to sort out some sort of interview sheet with which to question Theresa. She pored over all the information she had on her, trying to figure out the best angle. Rupert had given her a rough idea of the most suitable questions, but she had to make her own mark on the interview, make it her work. It had to project a warm image of Theresa, but that wouldn't be difficult, since Theresa was a very warm, if a little over-bubbly person.

It was six o'clock when she heard Jake's car pull up outside. She crept over to the window, looking out secretly from behind the lace curtain, her face hidden from view. The evening was still bright and sunny, touched with the languid warmth of a French summer.

'Home at last!' Melissa's gentle voice floated up to her in the stillness of the evening.

She heard Jake's soft laughter as he murmured something inaudible in reply. Melissa was smiling at Jake as she walked round to the front of the car, and Laura felt her heart contract as Jake slipped a casual arm around her and murmured something which made Melissa laugh, her voice soft and warm. They walked into the house together, still talking quietly.

Laura stood at the window for a long time, feeling bitter and hurt. So much for his denials! He was more than a friend to that woman – anyone with half an eye could see that at a glance. There was an indefinable closeness between them.

She wanted to cry. It was so unfair. She was stuck in this house with them for a week, and there was no way of avoiding them. She bit her lip. Melissa and Jake looked good together. Melissa was so utterly feminine, and Jake so completely male—the perfect couple, she thought, her lips twisting bitterly. Her eyes filled with tears, and she bit them back, her fists clenching by her sides. There was no room for tears. She would just have to put on a brave face. She would have to be very, very strong and ignore the jealousy and pain which welled up inside her every time she thought of Melissa with Jake.

CHAPTER EIGHT

LAURA had planned to interview Theresa the next morning. But this was made difficult owing to the fact that Theresa didn't get up until past eleven o'clock. Even then, she wandered around vaguely in a silk dressing gown, her face wearing a blank, slightly sulky expression.

'You really shouldn't let me sleep so late,' she complained to Russ. 'I always feel like this when I've had too much sleep. My head goes all thick and I feel heavy and tired.'

Russ watched her with an indulgent smile, his black eyes dancing. 'All right, pet, I'll bounce you out of bed at the crack of dawn tomorrow, how's that?'

Theresa looked horrified. 'Yuk!' she commented. 'I didn't mean that early. I meant something normal like nine-thirty. I have enough of early rising when I'm filming. All that running around at five o'clock in the morning can't be good for the soul, not to mention the digestion!'

Laura left them to it, closing the door behind her with an indulgent smile. They were obviously very close—it showed in every move they made, everything they said. It was good to see a happily married couple. Russ, for all his flirting, was devoted to his wife, and Theresa obviously felt the same way about him.

Not like me and Jake, Laura thought with a sigh as she wandered into the garden. The interview would have to wait until the afternoon, she thought with a shrug. That was a pity, because she had hoped to have it sewn up within two days or so. That would have given her a chance to get back to London as soon as possible.

She didn't think she would be able to stand seeing Jake and Melissa together for much longer. Every time she saw them, jealousy twisted inside her like a rusty knife, the pain making her wince while the poison filled her bloodstream.

'Miss Hadleigh!' a voice shrieked at her across the garden, and she turned round, looking back at the house. Mrs Winterbottom loomed in the front doorway, hands on hips, standing watching her.

She began to walk back. 'What is it, Mrs Winterbottom?' she called as she came closer to the house.

Mrs Winterbottom surveyed her with a disapproving face. 'There's a telephone call for you. I know it's long distance because I heard the pips as I picked it up.'

Laura frowned. 'Who is it? Did they say?'

Mrs Winterbottom gave her a nasty smile, her eyes knowing, her face like moulded dough. 'It was a man. Don't know what men are doing phoning you long-distance, I'm sure.'

Laura sighed as she reached the front door, and Mrs Winterbottom blocked the entrance. 'He didn't give a name?'

Mrs Winterbottom licked her lips. 'Said he was your boss. Didn't sound like anyone's boss to me, with that deep voice and all. If you ask me, he's just pretending.'

Laura sighed. 'Thank you, Mrs Winterbottom. I'm

sure he wasn't pretending.' She moved past her, and received a cross look from Mrs Winterbottom as she walked to the phone and picked it up.

'Hello?' she said, waiting for Rupert's voice.

'Oh, hello, Laura my dear,' Rupert blustered from hundreds of miles away, 'Rupert here.'

She smiled. 'Yes, I was told.'

Mrs Winterbottom lurked by the stairs, polishing the newel-post. Laura looked pointedly at her. She glowered back, then stomped off into the kitchen with a thwarted expression.

'What did you want to speak to me about, Rupert?' asked Laura as she turned back to the phone.

Rupert coughed. 'I just wondered how the interview was going. Got anything yet?'

Laura bit her lip. 'Well, I've made a start,' she lied.

'Oh, good, good,' Rupert blustered on. 'Well, keep up the good work, my dear. Er . . .' he paused, 'one more thing before I go. I thought I'd remind you that you must stay on for a week.'

Laura frowned. 'I already know that.'

Rupert coughed again. 'Yes, yes, I know, my dear. But there are going to be a lot of famous names there at the end of the week. Party, you see, to celebrate Theresa's new contract.'

Laura frowned. 'I didn't know anything about that. Nobody told me.'

Rupert laughed nervously. 'Didn't they? Oh well, never mind. Anyway, must be off now. Carly's just put her head round the door. Don't forget, we want you to report on the party. See you next week. 'Bye!'

'Rupert. . . .' Laura began, but the phone had gone dead. She stared at it as though she had only just discovered it in her hand and wondered what it was doing there.

Why had he sounded so worried? She could imagine him sitting behind his big oak desk, mopping his brow as he replaced the receiver. Nobody had told her about the party.

She frowned. Now she thought about it, she could remember Melissa saying something about her husband flying in for a party on Friday. But why had Rupert rung to remind her to stay on all week? As far as he knew, she had been intending to do just that anyway.

Her eyes narrowed. Jake! Jake had rung Rupert and told him to make sure she stayed on at the house all week. Her teeth clamped together with irritation. How dared he? She realised why he had done it, of course. He had thought he needed more time to break Laura down into listening to him and Melissa. He was so conceited that he thought it was only a matter of time before she gave in and believed what he was saying.

She leaned against the wall, mulling things over in her mind. She would have to have a word with Jake; tell him to stop interfering with her life.

She gave a little start as she heard the drawing room door open. Voices floated out to her, and she stood quite still, unable to stop listening, unable to move.

'Jake, we have to tell her.' Melissa's voice came through the door.

Laura stiffened, her heart beating with a slow, heavy thud as the words sank in.

She heard Jake give a deep sigh. 'Do you think I don't know that? I've tried so many times, Lissa, but she just makes it impossible for me.'

Laura's heart contracted as she heard the way he spoke her name. A tender nickname for Melissa—a biting fury every time he came near Laura. She bit her lip, wanting to get away so that she couldn't hear any more.

Melissa's gentle tones came through the open doorway. 'Perhaps I should speak to her. I know she hates me, but maybe she'll see things differently if it came from me rather than you.'

Jake sighed again. 'I don't know. Perhaps you're right. I just can't seem to think straight any more.'

'Poor darling,' Melissa said gently.

'It's not just what happened between us, you see,' Jake continued, his voice deep and troubled. 'It goes deeper than that. There's so much more behind it than what happened on our wedding day.'

'Her father?' Melissa prompted gently.

Laura's breath caught in her throat. Melissa knew! How could Jake do this to her? How could he discuss such painfully intimate details of her life with this woman?

'Yes,' his voice was crisp, 'that's why I have to tread so carefully with her. There are so many painful emotions running inside her that just one false move can trigger them off, and that's when she loses her temper, makes it impossible for me to talk to her.'

Melissa sighed softly. 'It's got to be said, Jake. You can't go on like this for ever.'

There was a silence. Then Jake said rawly, 'I know.' Laura heard him take a deep breath. 'It's killing me,' he said deeply.

Laura felt the tears prick her eyelids as she listened. What did he mean, it was killing him? She bit her lip as it trembled under the onslaught of pain. He wanted a divorce—that was what he must mean. Did he want a divorce in order to marry Melissa?

Laura shrugged. What did it matter who he wanted to marry? If Melissa was already married, he could hardly mean to marry her. But it didn't make much difference either way. If he wanted a divorce, it meant that she would lose him, and that hurt her more than anything she had ever experienced before.

Her heart lurched as she remembered the afternoon he had made love to her. Anger began to fill her, hurt pride and bitterness wiping away all the pain she had felt.

Jake had lain in her bed, held her in his arms, and all the time he had wanted to be with some other woman. She clenched her fists, her teeth coming together. How dared he do that to her? She felt sick, disgusted. She wanted to kill him so that no other woman would ever have him.

Her lips tightened. Rupert could go to hell. So could Jake. She wasn't hanging around here a minute longer. It was just too much to expect of her, she just wasn't strong enough to take it.

She pushed away from the wall.

'Someone's outside!' Melissa's panic-stricken voice came into the hallway.

The door was flung open just as Laura reached the foot of the stairs. She looked round, her eyes filled with anger as she stared at Jake.

She lifted her head with stiff pride. 'I heard.'

Jake studied her with hooded eyes, his face troubled. 'I see,' he said deeply.

'Yes, you see.' She gripped the banister unsteadily,

keeping her voice level. 'I want you to know that you're free to do whatever you please. There are no locks on my doors—there never have been. I don't give a damn what you do or who you do it with. You can have your divorce and you can have Melissa, or whoever it is you want. Good luck to the woman who gets you in the end. She'll soon find out what a cheat and a liar you are!' she was breathing jerkily as she spoke, trying desperately to control her feelings.

Jake's eyes widened, surprise flickering over his features. 'I think you've got something wrong somewhere, Laura,' he said slowly, frowning as he took a step towards her.

She kept her back straight, her eyes proud. 'No, Jake. The only time I ever got anything wrong about you was the day I married you. But,' she shrugged with a casual air which she was far from feeling, 'we all make mistakes. You're free to have your divorce whenever you want it.'

She turned her face away, beginning to walk up the stairs, her whole body stiff as she concentrated on getting away from him as coolly as possible.

'Wait!' His long legs carried him effortlessly up the stairs after her, his hand gripping her arm as he drew level with her. 'Where are you off to?'

She lifted her head. 'I'm going to my room.'

He watched her for a second, his face unreadable as the blue eyes glittered across her features. Then he shook his head. 'Oh no, you're not,' he told her. 'You're coming back downstairs to listen to what Melissa and I have to say.'

Anger flared in her, tears stinging the backs of her eyelids. He wasn't content with humiliating her in private—he wanted to humiliate her in front of Melissa as well. 'Didn't you hear what I said?' she demanded angrily. 'I don't give a damn what you and Melissa do. Leave me out of it, I'm not interested!'

A muscle jerked in his cheek. His hand tightened on her wrist while he studied her, his eyes angry as he exerted control over his temper. 'And what exactly,' he asked in a controlled voice, 'do you believe Melissa and I have in mind?'

Laura glared at him. 'Don't pretend innocence with me, Jake!' she muttered between her teeth. 'You and Melissa go a long way back—you told me so yourself. Frankly,' she glanced with hatred and contempt at Melissa, 'I'm surprised she's willing to have you. She's obviously a fool. Or perhaps she's just been taken in by your charm, the same way I was.'

Blue sparks flashed from his eyes, but he controlled his temper once more. 'What,' he asked tightly, 'is that meant to mean?'

She gave him a scathing look. 'Don't tell me you don't know, Jake. You give the impression of being tender, considerate and loving. You hide your thoughtlessness, your callousness until it's too late to escape the trap.'

'Don't be so melodramatic,' Jake said angrily. 'You always did have a taste for melodrama, but there's no need to use it on me.'

'I wouldn't say that.' She raised her eyebrows haughtily. 'I'd say there was every need. You think you know how to treat women. You think all it takes are empty words and red roses and you'll have us eating out of your hand.' She drew a deep breath. 'Well, you're wrong. Empty words can only ever be empty.

Treating a woman well is all about caring, and trusting and needing that one person.'

'Don't talk to me about trust!' he said tersely. 'Until you understand what you're talking about the best thing you can do is just be quiet.'

'I will not be quiet! Treating a woman well is all about saying what you mean and sticking to it. And you never do that, do you, Jake? Your promises are written in water. You're just like my father!'

His mouth firmed into a hard angry line. 'Not your bloody father again! I wish to hell you'd stop seeing everything through your mother's twisted eyes!'

Slivers of ice shot through her heart and she stared at him in silence for a painful moment. 'You bastard!' she breathed. 'How dare you!'

He frowned. 'Just give me a chance to explain, Laura. For God's sake stop running from the truth.'

'I will not give you a chance to explain!' she retorted in a painful whisper, breathing hard as anger came flooding back into her veins. 'Do you want to know why? Because I'm not interested. Do what you want with whom you want – just don't expect me to hang around waiting to hear all about it. I'm sick of your lies and your cheating.'

She began to walk away from him, shaking with anger. Her legs would go soon, she was sure, because the pain inside her was almost killing her.

A hand grasped her arm, and Jake stood beside her, his face stony, his eyes glittering. 'If you think I'm letting you walk away like this without talking it out, you're wrong!'

Laura's head turned slowly as she realised that Theresa and Russ had now come out and were standing at the bottom of the stairs watching with amazement and wicked curiosity.

She pulled her arm angrily away from Jake. 'You want to cause a scene, do you?' she asked between her teeth, her eyes flashing down to the people who were watching them.

Jake glanced over his shoulder at them. 'I don't give a damn what they hear,' he said tightly, turning back to her with a harsh, forbidding face.

Laura glared at him, humiliated and angry. 'Okay, you'll get your scene!' she hissed, 'and I hope you enjoy it!' And she struck out blindly, her lips clamped together as she pushed all her strength into her arm.

Her hand struck his cheek with force, and his head snapped back, leaving a look of manic fury on his face.

She stared at him in the tense, hostile silence for a brief second, then she ran up the stairs, her legs shaking, her movements jerky, her face tight. Jake caught up with her outside her room, and spun her to face him.

'What made you do that?' he ground out. 'Do you think it's going to make it any better by fighting in public?'

Anger shook her from her head right down to her toes. 'You conceited bastard,' she said jerkily, 'you really believe you can talk your way out of any situation, don't you? Well, think again! You can't talk your way out of this one!'

She whirled before he could stop her, slamming her bedroom door behind her and sliding the bolt home. She leant against the door breathlessly as he hammered on it, twisting the handle.

'Open this door!' he shouted.

Laura moved away from the wood panels, calling back, 'Go away, Jake. I don't want to speak to you again!'

He banged violently on the door. 'If you don't open this door, I'll break it down!' he threatened.

Laura tightened her lips, 'Go ahead!' she yelled back angrily.

From downstairs she heard the faint murmur of voices, filled with disbelief. Then there was a loud thud as Jake's foot hit the door, and she backed instinctively.

Two violent crashes followed the first, then came a splintering sound as the wood began to crack. Oh, my God, she thought wildly, her hand to her mouth, he's really going to break the door down!

The door crashed back on its hinges and Jake strode angrily into the room. She backed, her heart in her mouth, sensing the violence in him.

He towered over her, tall dark and menacing. 'Go downstairs,' he bit out.

Laura swallowed. 'No.'

There was a tense silence. Jake was so still that Laura felt fear rush through her with an icy chill.

'Go downstairs,' he repeated through clenched teeth.

She didn't have time to move before he caught her by the wrists and began to pull her towards the door. She struggled, but he was stronger, and she found herself half falling, half running down the stairs after him.

Her cheeks burnt with embarrassment as she tried to avoid the avid gazes of Russ and Theresa. Jake pulled her into the living room, slamming the door behind them. He watched her for a second, then he said in a clipped voice, 'Sit down.'

Laura clamped her lips together, but sat down, not daring to provoke him further by refusing. She glared at him, showing her anger with her eyes instead of her words.

Jake opened the door. 'Come in, Melissa.'

Melissa entered, her haunted face filled with sympathy as she studied Laura. She turned to look at Jake. 'Are you sure she's ready to hear us out?' she asked quietly.

Jake's narrow-eyed gaze fell on Laura, freezing her. 'She'll listen,' he told Melissa confidently, his face unyielding. 'Won't you?' His voice was dangerously soft as he looked back at Laura.

Laura eyed him obstinately, folding her arms and making up her mind not to believe a word they said. She was sick and tired of being pushed around just because he was stronger physically than she.

Jake and Melissa sat down opposite her. 'Okay, I'll start at the beginning,' said Jake. 'Melissa and I do go back a long way together. I knew her long before I ever met you.' He glanced at Melissa.

Laura watched the other woman with hatred. She didn't want to listen to this. Melissa nodded in reply, her silky black hair tumbling around her shoulders. 'Jake and I were thinking of getting married about a year before he actually met you.'

Laura stared at her. Poor woman, she thought, it must have been quite a shock to find out what kind of man he was.

Jake's eyes narrowed. 'Don't think I don't know what's going on inside that devious little mind of yours,' he told her. 'But you're wrong. I haven't got twenty other ditched wives hanging around the world, so you can get that idea straight out of your head now.'

Laura tried, and failed, to look offended. 'I didn't think anything of the sort,' she protested, mentally crossing her fingers.

Jake raised one disbelieving-eyebrow, but didn't make any further comment. 'We were seeing each other regularly for around a year. Gradually we seemed to drift towards the idea of marrying and settling down.' He shrugged broad shoulders. 'We were unattached, and over thirty, and we both thought it was time we married and began a family of sorts.' He looked across at Melissa with tenderness. 'But we were never deeply in love,' he said gently.

Melissa smiled softly. 'I know, Jake.' She looked at him for one more brief moment before turning her attention back to Laura. 'We decided to marry after I returned from India.'

'India?' Laura frowned. 'Why India?'

Jake took up the story. 'Melissa was working with a television documentary team at the time. They had to go out to India for six months on an important story. Naturally, we agreed that if we both still felt the same when she came back,' he spread his hands in front of him, 'we would marry.'

Melissa's tragic blue eyes smiled kindly at Laura. 'The trouble was that I moved around India so much with the team that Jake couldn't reach me with any of his letters.' She smiled again. 'He never knew whether I was in Delhi or Chandighar, and half the time I never knew where I was going to be either. We moved around so much, and sometimes we worked up to a dead end before realising the story was taking us elsewhere.'

Laura looked steadily at the floor. She was worried that she might be convinced by their story, and that frightened her. She didn't want any more humiliation.

Jake smiled at Melissa. 'Apart from that, the mail service in India is appalling.'

Laura gritted her teeth. 'How fascinating,' she murmured with deliberate boredom.

Jake's eyes narrowed on her coldly. 'Don't be so bloody rude,' he bit out in an icy voice. 'When I met you,' he continued a moment later, 'I tried to reach her. I sent telegrams, letters—I tried everything I could to get in touch with her and tell her about us. But it was no use.' He shrugged. 'I kept getting letters from her that indicated only that she hadn't heard from me.'

Laura raised her brows. 'This is all very sweet, but what does it have to do with me?'

'I'm getting to that,' he said tightly. 'When Melissa arrived back, it was the day of our wedding. She placed a call to my office, but I'd taken the day off, if you remember, to make sure everything was running according to plan.'

Laura looked away. She remembered, although she didn't want to. I wish he'd get this over with, she thought, irritated.

Melissa took up the story. 'I couldn't believe it when everybody told me he was getting married.' She made a face, shrugging. 'I'd been looking forward to getting back to him all the time I was in India. The work was tough, and I enjoyed it, but the only time we had to ourselves was at night when we'd finished work and gone to bed. Then I could think about Jake, and plan for our wedding.' She looked at the floor.

Jake sighed. 'I had no idea she was back in town,' the blue eyes were riveted on her, 'until she arrived at the wedding.'

Melissa's face was filled with worry as she looked at Laura. 'I had to see him,' she whispered into the silence.

Laura glanced away. Get on with it, she thought angrily as the first stirrings of compassion took root within her.

Melissa sighed softly. 'I didn't understand what was happening to the world I'd built up around him. I suppose I reacted the same way you did—the way any woman would. I was hurt, and angry. I felt used and humiliated.'

Jake watched her, an unspoken apology glimmering in his eyes. Laura's fists clenched. She could understand the way Melissa had felt, but that hardly excused the way he had treated her.

Melissa took a deep breath. 'I came to the wedding out of anger and, I suppose, a little masochism. I wanted to see what you looked like. I was going to shout at you, both of you.' She sighed. 'But I guess I'm just not built like that. I was a woman scorned, but I couldn't find the fury of hell in me. I went straight up to Jake's room when I knew he'd be alone.'

Laura eyed her bitterly. 'Why? Why did you do that, knowing the trouble it might cause? You must have realised what would happen if you went up there to see him alone in his bedroom.'

A deep strength filled the other woman's face. 'I was hurt and angry. I deserved an explanation.' She eyed

Laura steadily. 'He owed me at least that.'

Laura couldn't help but agree with her. She nodded slowly, averting her gaze and waiting until she spoke again.

Melissa looked down at her hands. 'I couldn't face you, Laura,' she said quietly. 'I knew I wouldn't be able to see you close up. Oh, I wanted to see what you looked like, I know—but I didn't want to speak to you. You were the enemy. You were the woman who'd taken Jake from me in six short months.'

Laura fought against the growing compassion inside her for Melissa. Was what they were saying true?

Melissa watched her steadily, then spoke in a voice that sounded almost wondering. 'I sat at the back of the church, watching you, listening to the smile in your voice, envying you, hating you, wishing Jake had never met you.'

There was a little silence, then Jake said, 'When she came to my room, I was stunned. I just didn't know what to say to her. She was so upset, so confused. It was as though she was walking around in a dream.' He frowned deeply, shaking his head. 'I tried to explain gently, but it was difficult. It's all very well saying that when you fall in love for real it happens too quickly for anyone to be able to do anything about it. But to apply that to the one you love when they've just left you is practically impossible to do.'

Laura saw his point. She frowned, sighing deeply. It sounded so real, so convincing. Were they telling the truth?

'I started to cry,' Melissa said in a whisper, then made a face, her voice becoming stronger. 'I feel rather foolish now, but at the time I thought I'd walked into a nightmare, and it was all I could do to stop screaming and breaking things.'

I know how you felt, thought Laura bitterly, recalling her trance-like state after the break-up.

'I didn't know quite what to do when she began to cry,' Jake said deeply. 'So I just followed my instincts and comforted her as best I could.'

Laura's eyes flicked to his face. 'You kissed her,' she said coldly.

A tide of deep red flowed up his face. 'I didn't intend to at first. I just put my arms around her. . . .' He broke off.

Melissa continued for him, seeing that it was difficult for him to explain. 'I needed him more then, you see, than I'd ever needed him. I knew he loved you very much, and I knew it was over between us. But I needed that last kiss. It just seemed so natural to turn my face to his and kiss him for the last time. The tears had stopped, and it was my way of saying goodbye. I guess Jake didn't want to reject me any more than he already had when it was so obvious that I needed him for the last time. He didn't want to hurt me.'

'So you hurt me instead,' Laura said to Jake with a trace of bitterness.

There was a little silence. 'I didn't want to,' said Jake in a raw, low voice. 'I never wanted to hurt you, Laura.'

Laura stood up. She wanted to get out of the room because she could feel the hot tears behind her lids and she didn't want Jake to see them. She believed their story, but she felt it was too late to go back, too late to try to recapture what they had.

'I've heard all this before,' she muttered, feeling confused and unsure.

Jake watched her for a second before standing up too. 'No, you haven't,' he said, 'because you never listened before.'

She stared at him, unable to speak. She felt guilty for putting them all through this mess, she felt sorry for Melissa, and she knew she had wronged both of them. But it went against all the anger and hatred she had built up over the last year. Was she weakening? She shivered. Or was she just growing up and opening her eyes?

Jake's eyes narrowed. 'You don't believe us, do you?' His voice was dangerously soft, and Laura felt the hair on the nape of her neck prickle.

Her eyes darted from Jake to Melissa and back again. They were watching her intently. She swallowed. 'It's a very touching story,' she heard herself say.

She bit her lip, wondering why she was talking like that. She knew how callous it must have sounded, how bitter it made her sound. She stared into Jake's angry eyes. What have I become? she thought dazedly. I'm only twenty-one and I'm already filled with bitterness and spite. She clenched her fists, wishing there was some way out of all this.

Her eyes registered Melissa's stricken look and she swallowed. Why had she said that? Melissa had just bared her soul, and all Laura could do was make callous remarks.

She drew her courage to her, turning to walk out of the room, but Jake's hand grasped her arm as she reached the door.

'You're not going anywhere,' he bit out.

She looked up at him. 'I'm not staying down here for another moment,' she said unsteadily.

Jake ignored her, turning instead to look at Melissa. 'Melissa, wait in the other room for us.'

Melissa walked past them with that tragic look in her huge blue eyes, and Laura's heart fell. Why had she deliberately hurt Melissa again? She was beginning to think of herself in a totally different light. Why, she asked herself frantically, can't I take things at face value? Learn to trust instead of suspect?

She didn't have time to think any more. Jake pulled her away from the door.

'I've had enough of you,' he grated. 'From now on you're going to change your ideas. We're going to get a few things straight between us.'

Laura bit her lip, then made a last attempt at courage. 'Is that so?' she asked.

'I've put up with your sharp little tongue, I've put up with your hang-ups about your father, and I've put up with your crazy bitterness. I'm not going to put up with any more. From now on you're going to have to learn to do as you're bloody well told!'

She glared at him. 'I'm sick of being pushed around. . . .' she began.

His hands pulled her towards him, bringing her closer so that her body brushed his with an electric sensuality which made her burn. 'Always the same old arguments, Laura. They can stop. You know exactly what happened between Melissa and me now, so don't think I'm going to take any notice of your outraged martyr act, because I'm not!'

'How dare you. . . .' she spluttered, irritated to hear him come so close to her own thoughts about herself.

'I dare very easily,' he said grimly. 'You're not a wronged woman, you're just a stupid one.'

Laura's mouth opened, but no words came out of it. She glared at him, saying the first thing that came into her head. 'Let go of me!'

'Not a chance,' he said. 'I let you go too often in the past. It's about time I showed you who's boss around here.'

'Why do you have to take such a high-handed attitude all the time?' she demanded, wriggling.

'High-handed?' He shook his head, 'I've been too gentle with you, I can see that. I felt sorry for you. That's my trouble—I feel sorry for too many people. I felt sorry for Melissa and look where that landed me. I felt sorry for you because your father had given you a raw deal—that's why I never tried to push it, never made you listen before. I didn't want to upset you.'

Laura glared at him indignantly. 'I didn't ask you to feel sorry for me!'

'I can see now that I should have taken a firm hand with you from the start,' he said, towering over her from what seemed like a great height. 'I can understand why you believed what you did. At the time it must have looked pretty damning. But you know now that what Melissa and I have just told you is the truth.'

She couldn't look at him. He was right. She knew they had told the truth, and felt guilty, stupid for not having listened before. It was so difficult to admit one had been wrong, however much one wanted to. It was also difficult to reformulate an opinion of someone close to you, to suddenly see them as a different person. Laura had spent a year hating Jake. Could she now see him with new eyes?

He pulled her nearer to him, their bodies hot against each other. His gaze dropped from her eyes to her mouth, burning on her lips as she gazed at him silently.

He looked back at her, and she felt his heart racing beneath the thin silk of his shirt. 'How do you make me feel like this, Laura?' he asked thickly. 'You've caused me nothing but endless trouble, but it's all I can do to keep my hands off you.'

Heat ran through her cheeks. 'It goes deeper than that for me, Jake. There can never be anything between us if all you want to do is have sex with me. If I don't feel emotion on both sides, you'll only make me very unhappy.'

He watched her from beneath hooded lids. 'Do you think it's that different for me? Don't you think sex without love seems empty to me? God, I can't even remember faces, let alone names. I often wonder what the point of it all is, but at the time there's one hell of a point! It's afterwards that everyone feels a little sad.'

'You don't understand what I'm saying,' she told him, feeling anger returning to her. 'I'm not getting involved with you again. I'm not going to risk it. You may be able to turn me on, but that just isn't enough.'

His face was unreadable, his eyes hooded by heavy lids. 'That wasn't what I was offering you,' he said deeply.

Laura pulled back. 'Wasn't it? I got the feeling you wanted me back only to have me in your bed at nights. Well, I don't want to now. Desire runs thin if it's satiated too often. I'd be frightened that one morning I'd wake up to find another woman in your bed.'

Jake looked perplexed, frowning. 'What are you talking about?'

She looked at him steadily. 'Someone once said, "To love is nothing, To be loved is something, To love and be loved is everything." That's me, Jake. I don't want anything you can offer me, because I need to love and be loved.'

His brows jerked together. 'You're crazy. . . .' he began.

'Don't make fun of me!' she interrupted angrily. 'It's the way I'm made, and you can't change it. I'm not interested in casual sex with you or anyone.' She took a deep breath. 'I don't want to ever see you again.'

His eyes blazed. 'But you love me!'

Tears stung the back of her eyes. 'Yes,' she said tautly, holding her head straight. 'I love you, although God knows why. But that doesn't make any difference, you see—I can't face the thought of a one-sided marriage. I want to be loved by you, not just desired.'

He laughed softly. 'Oh, I see. Not just a sex object, is that it?'

Her eyes flashed. 'Don't make fun of me, Jake. . . .' she began.

Jake placed one long finger over her mouth. 'Not another word,' he murmured, his face coming closer to hers until she felt his breath fan her cheek.

'Will you just let go of me?' she said shakily.

He shook his head, the thick black hair brushing softly against her neck. 'Not a chance. I love you too much to ever be able to let go of you again.'

Laura's heart stopped for one incredulous moment. She lifted her head, not daring to breathe in case she had heard wrong. 'What did you say?' she asked, and her voice was strained with the pain of fear of rejection.

Jake's eyes flicked to her face. 'I said, I love you,' he murmured deeply against her mouth.

Joy shot through her as they stared at one another in silence. He had never said he loved her before, and she could hardly contain the lightheaded relief.

He brushed her mouth with his. 'Come back to me, Laura. My life has been one long lonely series of grey unbearable moments of agony since you left.'

She stared up at him. 'So has mine.'

'I need you,' he whispered, his mouth making her heart stir as it moved sensuously against hers.

'How can I be sure?' she asked in a hushed, breathless voice. 'How can I be sure you love me enough?'

He stopped kissing her, looking down at her with serious eyes. 'You can't,' he said deeply, and her heart fell. 'You can never be that sure of anything in life. All you can do is trust me. Give me your trust, Laura, and I'll give you everything I have, everything I can possibly give.'

Could she do that? It seemed such a little thing to ask. She looked at him with new eyes, seeing the love in his face, the hope in his eyes that told her he needed her, and her heart surged upwards. All her life she had been looking for this man—someone stronger than her who would love her, look after her, make her feel needed and safe, and now she had found him. Hold on to him, a little voice inside her said.

She smiled up at him tremulously. 'I trust you,' she said on a whisper.

Relief surged into his face, his gaze softening as he drew her back to him, his arms closing around her with gentle yet firm finality.

'I want to build my life around you,' he murmured as his mouth brushed hers. 'I'll make you feel so safe you'll never want to leave again.'

His mouth moved hotly over hers, the kiss slow and sensual as his arms tightened on her, his hands caressing her softly, making the sweet, honeyed excitement more exquisite. Then he drew back, his eyes glinting as he looked down at her. 'I want you in my bed every night,' he murmured, 'I want to wake up to find your hair spilling on to my pillow.'

Laura smiled. 'I'll be there.'

His eyes flicked hotly over her. 'I want to fill you up with sons,' he said thickly. Then he groaned, gathering her into his arms again and kissing her until her head spun and she found herself clinging to him helplessly.

There was a loud cough from the doorway, and Laura and Jake turned slowly, looking towards the door with stunned looks on their faces. Russ stood watching them with a wickedly curious look in his black eyes.

'Hello,' he said, grinning. 'We thought we'd better hang around in case you murdered her.'

Jake allowed a smile to curve his lips. 'I'm not in the habit of murdering my wife.' He glanced at Laura. 'However maddening she can be at times!'

An evil grin flickered on Russ's face. 'Mr and Mrs John Smith, eh?' he said, not realising that Jake was serious. 'Don't worry, your secret is safe with me. Shan't tell a soul, I promise.'

Jake raised an eyebrow. 'Tell whoever you like,' he said with amusement, 'but get the name right—it's Mr and Mrs Jake Ashton.'

Russ looked unsure of himself for a second, then he grinned again. 'Well, congratulations seem to be in order. When's the happy day?'

Jake smiled at Laura. 'You missed it. We've been married for a year now. We're just celebrating our first anniversary, aren't we, darling?'

Laura smiled shyly from beneath her lashes. 'Yes, I suppose we are,' she said softly.

Russ gaped in astonishment. 'Who would have believed it? I always said you were a dark horse, Jake, but I didn't realise you were this bad. Talk about secretive!' He shook his head with amused disbelief.

Jake smiled into Laura's eyes. 'They say the first year is the hardest,' he murmured, 'and the years that follow are the happiest.'

A frown creased Laura's brow, worried by what Jake had said, now totally unaware of Russ, who still stood in the doorway watching them. She bit her lip.

'But what if they aren't, Jake?' she said quietly.

He kissed her softly. 'They will be,' he promised.

And they were.

Harlequin Plus

THE MYSTICAL ISLE OF MAN

It is little wonder that Sarah Holland was inspired to write her delightful romance, *Tomorrow Began Yesterday*. For Sarah Holland, one of Harlequin's newest writers, lives on the Isle of Man, a mystical romantic place of inspirational beauty and folklore in the Irish Sea.

First settled by the Celts, then conquered by the Vikings, the Isle of Man owes its romantic atmosphere to these ancient founding races. On a tour of the thirty-mile-long island it is not unusual to come across the remains of their round dwellings, runic crosses and monuments. Even the Celts' lilting language, which is related to Gaelic, is still spoken by a few Manx, as the residents are called. But perhaps the best legacy from the past are the stories of the island's magical inhabitants, the "little people," of whom there are two types: the *phynnodderee*—the wicked little people—recognized by their hairy faces and bright eyes; and the *mooinjer-ny-gioneveggey*, the good little people. Usually dressed in green with red caps, the latter can be found dancing in glens or splashing in waterfalls. Their benevolent nature, however, lasts only until someone does them insult or injury, such as calling them fairies, a term these sturdy little folk especially scorn.

Perhaps Sarah might one day give us the pleasure of setting a romance on this mystical island!

The bestselling epic saga of the Irish. An intriguing and passionate story that spans 400 years.

FIRST...
The Defiant

Lady Elizabeth Hatton, highborn Englishwoman, was not above using her position to get what she wanted ... and more than anything in the world she wanted Rory O'Donnell, the fiery Irish rebel. But it was an alliance that promised only ruin....

THEN...
The Survivors

Against a turbulent background of political intrigue and royal corruption, the determined, passionate Shanna O'Hara searched for peace in her beloved but troubled Ireland. Meanwhile in England, hot-tempered Brenna Coke fought against a loveless marriage....

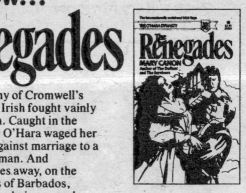

Romance Treasury

Your chance
to collect
beautiful early editions!

Each Romance Treasury volume is a
delightful anthology of three favorite
Harlequin Romances all by bestselling
authors of romantic fiction. Handsomely
bound in gold-embossed leatherette
hard covers, with colorfully illustrated
jackets, these attractive volumes are
an asset to any home library!

Choose from the list of great volumes
on the following page.

Choose from this list of
Romance Treasury editions

**Complete and mail coupon
on following page today!**

Collect a love-story library with
Romance Treasury

Complete and mail this coupon today!

Harlequin Reader Service

In the U.S.A.   In Canada
1440 South Priest Drive   649 Ontario Street,
Tempe, AZ 85281   Stratford, Ontario N5A 6W2

Please send me the following Romance Treasuries. I am enclosing
my check or money order for $6.97 for each Treasury ordered plus
75¢ to cover postage and handling.

☐ *Volume 8*	☐ *Volume 62*
☐ *Volume 11*	☐ *Volume 65*
☐ *Volume 43*	☐ *Volume 68*
☐ *Volume 49*	☐ *Volume 71*
☐ *Volume 54*	☐ *Volume 75*

Number of Treasuries checked @ $6.97 each = $_____

N.Y. and Ariz. residents add appropriate sales
tax. $_____

Postage and handling $_____ 75¢

I enclose   TOTAL $_____

(Please send check or money order. We cannot be responsible for cash sent through
the mail.)
Prices subject to change without notice.

NAME_____

ADDRESS_____
                                          (APT. NO.)
CITY_____

STATE/PROVINCE_____

ZIP/POSTAL CODE_____
Order while quantities last. This offer expires April 30, 1983   21056000000